LOVE

"I've got to find Eileen a date for the Alpha Delt formal," Bess said to Paul, twirling the phone cord with her hand. "And it's not as easy as it seems. She's pretty particular. He's got to be a cut above the average guy. You know, good-looking, athletic but sensitive, but not muscle-bound."

"Oh, so is that all the use you have for me?" Paul joked into the phone. "Paul Cody, date finder."

"Of course you know it's not." Bess laughed. "But this is important. Do you know anyone?"

"I'm thinking, I'm thinking," Paul said.

Just then Paul's towering roommate, Emmet Lehman, walked into their room. He was wearing his Wilder Norsemen football jacket, with a white shirt and neat crewneck sweater under it.

"Paul?" Bess said. "You still there?"

Suddenly Paul smiled, and he put the phone close to his ear.

"Bess, I think I just found the answer to Eileen's dilemma," he said. "Your worries are over."

Nancy Drew on Campus™

Available from ARCHWAY Paperbacks

Nancy Drew
on campus ™ #13

Campus

Exposures

Carolyn Keene

AN ARCHWAY PAPERBACK
Published by POCKET BOOKS
New York   London   Toronto   Sydney   Tokyo   Singapore

This book is a work of fiction. Names, characters, places and incidents are products of the author's imagination or are used fictitiously. Any resemblance to actual events or locales or persons, living or dead, is entirely coincidental.

AN ARCHWAY PAPERBACK *Original*

An Archway Paperback published by
POCKET BOOKS, a division of Simon & Schuster Inc.
1230 Avenue of the Americas, New York, NY 10020

Copyright © 1996 by Simon & Schuster Inc.
Produced by Mega-Books, Inc.

ISBN: 0-671-56802-7

First Archway Paperback printing September 1996

10 9 8 7 6 5 4 3 2 1

NANCY DREW, AN ARCHWAY PAPERBACK and colophon are registered trademarks of Simon & Schuster Inc.

NANCY DREW ON CAMPUS is a trademark of Simon & Schuster Inc.

Cover photos by Pat Hill Studio

Printed in the U.S.A.

IL 8+

Campus
Exposures

CHAPTER

"Ned? It can't be!" Nancy Drew gasped in disbelief as she caught a glimpse of a guy rushing past her in the crowded hall of the Hewlitt Performing Arts Center. Nancy had wandered over to the arts complex after her Thursday afternoon classes to pick up a schedule for the Focus Film Society's movie screenings. Now all thoughts of the film society were dashed from her head as she stared blankly at the space where seconds before her ex-boyfriend, Ned Nickerson, had been.

"What is Ned doing here at Wilder?" Nancy asked out loud as she felt herself being bumped and jostled by other students. Suddenly she felt ridiculous standing and staring at nothing in the middle of a jammed hallway. Nancy started moving again.

All right, get a grip and think this through, Nancy told herself sternly as she made her way to the small theater in the arts complex where the film society held its screenings.

That guy wasn't Ned—he had light brown hair. You've been putting in some big-time hours studying, so you're just sleep deprived, Drew. And for some reason you've got Ned on the brain and you're letting your imagination kick into overdrive.

When Nancy reached the theater, she took a film schedule from a rack outside the door. After settling into a chair in a corner grouping in the hallway, she began browsing through the list of films. Soon she'd forgotten about Ned and had started circling screenings she thought she'd like to attend.

"Hello." A deep, masculine voice floated through to her brain, breaking her concentration. Nancy's head snapped up, and she found herself peering up into a familiar face. She nearly jumped. The same guy she had spotted in the hall earlier was staring down at her. Nancy felt a powerful jolt surge through her. Ned— with light brown hair! She closed her eyes, then reopened them quickly.

The owner of the voice was tall and good-looking, who did resemble Ned very closely. He had the same angular facial structure, strong jaw, and athletic build. He was also tall, over six feet, just like Ned. Nancy struggled to find something to say.

"Uh—h-hi," she stammered.

The guy smiled easily. "I see you're interested in the Focus Film Society."

Nancy fought to regain her poise. "Well, yes. I don't know that much about classic films, but I want to learn," she admitted, wondering if her voice was shaking. "I've been to one screening, and I really enjoyed it. So I've decided to go more often."

"Well, you've picked a good time to check out FFS," the guy said. "We're sponsoring a film festival this weekend. If you've got a minute, I can tell you all about it." He shrugged and indicated the noisy hallway jammed with people. "It might be quieter if we sat in a corner of the lobby."

"That'd be great," Nancy said, smiling. Forget studying; forget the library, she thought as they threaded their way through the crowds.

"By the way, my name's Terry. Terry Schneider," the guy said.

"Nancy Drew," Nancy answered. "Have you been involved with the group for long?"

"I help run it," Terry said, seating himself on a bench in the lobby and making room for Nancy. "I don't think I've seen you at any of our screenings."

"I came last week for the first time," Nancy said. "I don't remember seeing you there." She didn't add that she'd definitely have noticed him.

"I had a big English paper due," Terry said.

"I think it was the first time I missed all semester. Anyway, let me tell you about the festival that starts this weekend. Have you ever heard of Sebastian Fletcher?"

Nancy frowned. "The name sounds vaguely familiar, but I'm not sure. Who is he?"

Terry leaned forward. "Well, you've heard of Sean Fletcher, haven't you?"

"The actor? Who hasn't?"

"Sebastian Fletcher was his father. He was a pretty big director in his day."

"I don't think I know about him," Nancy said.

"You've probably heard of his films though. He made a bunch of movies in the sixties that are popular cult films today—*Voyage Beyond, Candlelight Vigil.* We're screening *Road to Nowhere* on Friday. That's his most famous."

"I have heard of that one," Nancy said. "But I've never seen it."

"Then you have to come on Friday. Sean's going to be here to introduce the film. And I had to work really hard to get him. He usually distances himself from his dad's work, but this film is special. It's one of only a few films his mother, the actress Lauren Fletcher, had a part in."

"Wow, I can't believe you actually got him to come to Wilder. That's great," Nancy said.

"The art director, Robert Delucca, and one

of the actresses, Erika Swann, will be here, too. And so will you, I hope."

"Are you kidding? I wouldn't miss it," Nancy replied. Especially not after meeting you, she thought. She ran her fingers through her reddish blond hair and flipped it behind her shoulders. She stood reluctantly. "I guess I'd better head out. Thanks for telling me all this, Terry."

"My pleasure," Terry said, smiling warmly. "You're sure you'll be there?"

Nancy nodded and saw the invitation in Terry's eyes. "I promise."

"See you then," Terry said. He turned and disappeared into the crowd, leaving Nancy wondering if she'd only imagined him.

Bess Marvin stood in the wings waiting for her cue to go onstage. She and several other members of the theater department were finishing up a rehearsal for a one-act play in a series of one-acts the theater department would be opening soon. Bess watched Brian Daglian—in character—sit heavily in a folding chair center stage. Bess hurried onstage and crossed quickly in front of Brian.

"I wondered when, and if, you'd turn up," she said, reading her lines from the script.

"Oh, I always turn up," Brian read, using a smug tone of voice for his character.

"Cut!" yelled the student director. "Bess,

too soon. Too soon! You've got to give Brian time to settle in his chair and glance furtively around the room. He needs a chance to establish his character here."

"Sorry," Bess said as she went back to the wings to start again. This time she stumbled the tiniest bit over her line.

"That wasn't great either," she said. "Can we take it from the top one more time?"

"You bet," Brian said easily. "We'll take it as many times as we need."

Bess was grateful that Brian was as much a perfectionist as she was when it came to the stage. They both knew that attitude was what it took to deliver a top-notch performance. The next try was better, but still not perfect.

Finally, after another false start, everything went seamlessly. Bess's timing was flawless, and she delivered her lines precisely. Brian played off her perfectly. Now the story and characters came to life as she and Brian read through the next two scenes. When they stopped, they both said, "Wow, you were great," at exactly the same moment.

Bess laughed. No doubt about it, she decided. These one-act plays were going to be hits. She could feel it in her bones.

The director laid down his clipboard. "That was terrific. Let's quit on a high note. Be at rehearsal tomorrow at one-thirty sharp."

Bess picked up her backpack and said goodbye. Slowly, she headed toward the rear exit of the theater, still savoring the warm feeling of her performance. Suddenly Bess's eye fell on the clock hanging next to the light box.

"Uh-oh," she moaned. She'd made a date to meet Eileen O'Connor, a Kappa sorority sister, who was also one of Nancy's suitemates at Thayer Hall, Nancy's dorm. Bess was already a half hour late. She'd gotten so caught up in rehearsal, she hadn't paid the least attention to the time.

Glancing at her watch, Bess groaned, and after leaving the complex, broke into a run across the quad, nearly sideswiping several students. A few minutes later she'd arrived at the dorm, and was standing breathlessly in front of the door to Suite 301.

She knocked, and the door was opened by Liz Bader, one of Eileen and Nancy's suitemates. "Hi, Liz. Hi, everybody," Bess said, as she walked into the lounge. Several women were there, studying. Liz, an architecture major, went back to a small architectural foam model she was constructing.

Kara Verbeck, Nancy's roommate, glanced at Bess from her sprawled-out position on the smooshy sofa. Her eyes were bloodshot, and she closed her thick textbook. "Hey, Bess." She rubbed her eyes. "Welcome to study hell."

Eileen looked up from the notes she'd been poring over on the low coffee table. "Oh, hi."

"Eileen, I'm so sorry I'm so late," Bess said.

"Don't worry about it. I needed the extra study time," Eileen said.

"Don't remind me," Bess groaned. "Exam week is coming up."

"Well, at least we have something to look forward to before our brains are drained of every neuron they ever possessed," Kara said.

The women looked at one another and chorused: "Party!"

Bess's spirits did a quick rebound. Her sorority, Kappa, and the Alpha Delt fraternity were joining forces to host a formal party. Daniel Frederick, who was Liz's boyfriend, and Kara's boyfriend, Tim Downing, had told them that the Alpha brothers had reserved the banquet room in the most elegant restaurant in town, Les Peches. The Kappa sisters had booked the hottest campus band so there was no doubt the food and music were going to be great. Bess couldn't wait for the chance to dress up, have fun, and forget about classes and exams. Everyone started chattering about what they would wear and who would be there, but Bess noticed that Eileen wasn't taking part in the conversation.

"You okay?" Bess asked her.

Eileen shrugged. "I'm fine. It's just that once again, another party is upon us, and here I am, the Incredible Dateless Wonder."

Kara sat up. "Come on, Eileen, that's not a

problem. Give us a few hours. We'll find you a date."

Eileen shook her head, and a lock of sun-streaked blond hair fell over her forehead. "Thanks, but no thanks. To tell you the truth, I think I'm becoming seriously allergic to the whole dating thing. I mean, either I like a guy and he doesn't like me. Or one likes me, and I have no interest in him. It's totally depressing."

"You're not the first person who's felt like that," Bess said. "But then the time comes when everything clicks." Bess thought of her own incredible boyfriend, Paul Cody. She had never really believed it could happen either.

Eileen rolled her eyes. "Well, nothing's clicking for me. I've had it. I hereby give up on romance."

"Forget about it," Bess said. "We won't let you."

"Oh, yeah? Just watch me," Eileen said dryly. "I can't wait to curl up with a good video while you guys are worrying about what to wear."

"You can't be serious, Eileen," Kara said.

"And besides," Bess went on, "you've already won the Best Dressed award. That dress you let Stephanie buy for you is gorgeous. You can't let it go to waste."

"Bess is right," Liz said. "It's a violation of university policy to own a dress like that and not wear it to the party of the year." She and Kara looked at Bess, then back at Eileen. "Leave it to us. We have three good, if slightly study-worn, brains among us. We'll find the perfect guy for you."

Eileen laughed. "Okay. I can't wait to meet him. My heart's in your hands, guys. Come on, Bess. I'm not studying one more minute. Let's get out of here!"

Stephanie Keats stood before the glass doors of Berrigan's Department Store and gloomily studied the window displays. There were at least three outfits that she'd love to buy, but the problem was, for the first time in her life, Stephanie had no money, thanks to her dad, R. J., and that conniving witch of a stepmother, Kiki. Stephanie's dad had cut off all her credit cards, except one. And she'd run that one up to the limit. So how was a girl supposed to get by? Sure, she had her allowance. But it was so small, it hardly counted. There was no way she could afford nice clothes and cosmetics and all the things she was sure she had to have.

"I can't believe I'm being forced to do this," she muttered as she dropped her cigarette butt and ground it into the sidewalk angrily with her heel. Heaving a deep sigh, Stephanie finally stepped on the mat of the automatic door and entered the store.

It was absolutely not fair, she told herself,

dragging herself up the aisles. She should be shopping here, not getting ready to work as a part-time sales associate. Was that degrading, or what? Still, it wasn't as though she had much choice. She had finally located this job through Wilder's placement office, and today was the first day of employee training.

Like I need to be trained. As if any monkey couldn't handle being a sales drudge, Stephanie grumbled to herself. She paused to look at the notes she'd written at her interview: "Personnel Office, third floor. See Mrs. Caldwell."

"Hey, Stephanie, nice to see you."

Stephanie's head snapped up at the sound of the familiar voice. It was Pam Miller, a Wilder University student who roomed with Nancy's friend George Fayne in Jamison Hall. An athletic type—Stephanie had no use for her. Pam was standing behind a cosmetics counter and was waving at Stephanie.

Stephanie gazed right through Pam. *If she thinks I'm going to do a working-girl-togetherness thing, she's completely mistaken.* Stephanie turned her back on Pam and started toward the personnel office.

Ginny Yuen tilted her face toward the late afternoon sun and slowly rolled her shoulders to relieve a muscle cramp in her neck. She'd been in a lecture hall for hours, and it felt good to be outside walking to her dorm. Shifting her backpack, she continued moving her shoulders. Suddenly, she felt herself swept up in a full-body hug. Her nostrils filled with the familiar scent of her boyfriend Ray Johansson's aftershave.

"Ray!" she exclaimed happily. "What are you doing here? I thought you had class."

Ray grinned. "I do. So I'll be a little late. But I couldn't wait. I had to spill the news right now." Ray pulled Ginny close to him and kissed her on the tip of her nose.

"What news?" Ginny asked. "Tell me!"

Ray hugged her again. "The best news ever. It happened! It's official. Pacific Records has offered the Beat Poets a recording contract!"

Ginny caught her breath. "Oh, wow. When?"

"I just got the call," Ray said. "And I ran out to find you."

Now it was Ginny's turn to sweep Ray up in a monstrous hug. "I'm so happy for you. You deserve it. All the guys do."

"Thanks," Ray said. "We're all pretty excited. I think I'll have some serious trouble paying attention to classes today."

Ginny laughed. "I'll bet."

Ray drew Ginny up close. "Do you realize what this means? This is just the beginning for the Beat Poets. MTV, the Grammys, the Rock and Roll Hall of Fame—we're on our way!"

CHAPTER 2

Jake Collins stared at the blank computer screen on his desk. He had a paper due the next day, and the words just weren't flowing.

He thumbed through his notes for what seemed like the thousandth time and sighed with relief when he heard the doorbell ring. He needed a distraction. He jumped up and opened the door. "Nancy!" he said, "How did you know I was just getting ready for a break? And you're just the person I want to spend it with."

Nancy's sky blue eyes were set off by the soft, pale blue sweater she was wearing. Her reddish blond hair cascaded over her shoulders, and her lips were turned up in an enticing smile.

Jake cleared his throat. "Come on in," he said, stepping back to allow Nancy to enter.

"Am I disturbing you?" she asked.

Jake shook his head. "No way. This is just what I need right now."

Nancy moved some books and sat down on a chair by Jake's desk. "I just wanted to invite you to come with me tomorrow night to see a Sebastian Fletcher film called *Road to Nowhere*. It's part of a film festival of Fletcher's movies that the film society is sponsoring. I just wondered if you wanted to catch it with me."

Jake was tempted. After all, he could never get enough of Nancy. But he shook his head. "Thanks, but no thanks. I've got a ton of work to do. I'm not really a Fletcher fan anyway. Are you going to dress up?"

Nancy looked surprised. "Dress up? What are you talking about?"

"*Road to Nowhere* is a cult film. Most of the people who attend dress up in sixties hippie clothes like the characters in the movie. They wear wigs and makeup and bring all kinds of props. They turn the whole thing into a kind of audience participation fest, yelling back at the characters on the screen, singing along with the songs in the movie. It's wild."

"Hmmm. Sounds interesting," Nancy said. "I wonder why the guy from the film society didn't tell me about that."

Jake grinned. "He was probably saving it as a surprise. Sorry if I ruined it. You'll have a great time. Wish I could come."

Nancy shrugged. "Next time."

"Hey, how's your profile on the reclusive Mrs. Vandenbrock going?" Jake asked, referring to Nancy's assignment for her Journalism I class. The students had been given an assignment to write a personal profile on a historic or prominent citizen of Weston. Nancy had chosen the wealthy widow of one of the founding fathers of the city.

Nancy sighed. "Not so good."

"What's going on?" Jake asked.

"Well, I didn't get much further than the front door," Nancy said.

"What was it like?" Jake asked. "I've always wanted to see what was behind the imposing stone walls of that mansion."

"Well, I only saw behind them for a few minutes," Nancy said, "I started out with questions about her husband. The second I asked Mrs. Vandenbrock about herself she totally shut down. She didn't want to participate in a profile about herself. She said she had misunderstood and thought I was going to be writing about her husband. She had me escorted out in a flash." Nancy sighed again. "I didn't get enough information to finish my assignment."

"You're resourceful, Nan. You'll think of something," Jake replied.

"I don't want to give up, that's for sure," Nancy said firmly. "I thought about starting over with someone else, but I'm running out of time. The assignment's due pretty soon. And all this on top of exams."

"That's university life for you," Jake said with a shake of his head. "Pressure piled upon pressure."

"Deadline upon deadline," Nancy said, glancing over at Jake's computer screen.

"What do you say we just chuck it all?" Jake said, grabbing her hand and looking deep into her eyes. "I could run away with you."

"We could just toss our books and computers in the river and be free," Nancy added, warming to the theme.

Jake nodded. "You got it. Then we could jam a few things in our backpacks and head out across the country. We'd live off the land, follow the open road, go wherever we want, do whatever we feel like. No deadlines. No exams. How about it?"

"Sounds great," Nancy said. "But can I bring my computer?"

Jake pretended to look disappointed. "So you care more for that miserable bundle of microchips than you do for me?"

"No," Nancy replied. "I didn't say that. Come on, let's go."

Jake smiled and studied Nancy's face for a moment. If she were serious, he would be out the door with her in a flash. He found his eyes wandering over the graceful slope of her neck, taking note of the way her hair curled softly around her shoulders. Then he realized he could think of a better, more immediate way of relieving the pressures of college life. And he wouldn't even have to leave his room. Leaning over, he pulled Nancy into his arms, and his lips found their way to hers.

"Meeting adjourned."

Bess Marvin stood up after Kappa's meeting and talked with a few of her sorority sisters as she slowly made her way to the front door. That night's meeting had been interesting, and she wouldn't have minded sticking around to talk a little more, but she had promised she'd go to the Underground, an on-campus cafeteria during the day and music club at night. Bess and some Kappas were going there to hear the Beat Poets.

It had been just after Bess's last class of the day when Ginny had excitedly broken the great news about the Beat Poets' record deal. Then Ginny had mentioned that the band would be playing at the Underground that night. So Bess, Casey Fontaine, and Eileen had promised to go to the popular campus hangout that evening.

"Forget about exams. Where the Beat Poets are, so am I. It's time to celebrate," Casey had declared.

As soon as Eileen, Casey, and some of the other Kappa sisters who'd decided to come along had converged at the front door, Bess and her friends left the sorority house and made their way over to the Underground.

As they opened the door of the club, they could hear the distinctive sound of the Beat Poets. Spider and Bruce, two of the band members, raised their instruments in salute as Bess and her friends stepped inside the club.

Bess quickly found Ginny sitting at a table near the stage, along with several girls from Nancy's suite. She was surprised to see that Stephanie was also at the table. Normally, Stephanie turned up her nose at gatherings like this, declaring herself too sophisticated to hang out with the "childish college crowd."

I guess everyone loves a winner, even Stephanie, Bess said to herself as she trooped over to the table. She couldn't resist needling her, however. She squeezed in next to Stephanie, took note of her slinky black halter dress, and asked sweetly, "What brings you here? The sweet smell of success?"

"I needed an antidote to the dreary middle-America atmosphere of Berrigan's," Stephanie admitted almost cheerfully.

"Too much shopping, huh?" asked Eileen.

Stephanie's mouth set in a thin line. "Not exactly. I decided to get a job there. Just for fun. Something to do." She shrugged and started tapping her fingers in time to the sounds of the band's newest song.

Bess studied Stephanie closely. Weird, she thought. She'd heard that Stephanie had been cut off from her credit cards, but she hadn't actually thought Stephanie would become desperate enough to get a job.

Still, she didn't have time to worry about Stephanie's problems. Not when everyone was buzzing excitedly about the Beat Poets' record deal and all the possibilities that went with it. Ginny looked proud, and she led the applause after the band's first set.

The Underground was beginning to fill up. More and more people pulled up chairs to the table where Bess and her friends were sitting. First Liz Bader and Kara arrived. A little while later George Fayne strolled in with her boyfriend, Will Blackfeather. They sat down at a table nearby.

They're definitely the best-looking couple here, Bess thought happily. It was nice to see her cousin so happy with such a perfect guy.

"Hey, George, Will, over here," Bess called loudly, to be heard above the music.

George turned, and her face lit up when she spotted Bess. She got up and walked over to the group. Will followed, the dim light reflecting off his finely chiseled face.

"We decided we were overdue for a study break," George said happily. Will pulled up a chair, and she sat in his lap.

"Looks like lots of others had the same

idea," Bess said as Daniel and Tim and some other Alpha Delts showed up. They shoe-horned themselves in next to Liz and Kara.

Kara pounced on them instantly. "Anything new about the party?" Bess heard her ask.

"Well, we talked a little more about it at our meeting tonight," Tim said.

Instantly everyone clamored to hear more.

"No big news really, but it looks like we'll have a huge turnout," Daniel added.

Bess jumped in. "That's great. And the band's been confirmed. We're going to have a total blast."

While people continued to talk about the Alpha-Kappa party, however, Bess became aware that once again Eileen was frowning. Uh-oh. Danger sign, she thought.

Bess waited until she could talk to Eileen without being overheard by everyone else. "Have you changed your mind about the party?" she asked, trying to sound nonchalant. She didn't want Eileen to think she was being pushy.

Eileen shook her head. "There's nothing to change my mind about. No handsome princes have been falling at my feet begging me to go with them."

Bess snorted. "That's the only thing stop-ping you?"

"You've heard my reasons, and they haven't changed," Eileen said loudly. Bess noticed that several of the women at the table had turned in her direction.

"But, Eileen, think about how you'll feel if you miss it. Everyone will be talking about it," Bess said.

Eileen shook her head. "You know, the more I think about formal parties, the more I'm against them. Why should people have to go to so much trouble to dress up just to please a date? I'm actually thinking of trying to organize an *in*formal event for that night. To give people a choice. People like me who are allergic to dating. I'm thinking of something like, say, maybe an in-line skating party. An activity where you don't need a date to have fun."

"Eileen, there are tons of informal events held all the time around campus," Liz said. "You can skate any time."

"Oh, Eileen, come on," Casey joined in. "You've got to come to the formal."

Eileen frowned. "What I've *got* to do is get a soda," she replied, then hurried off. George and Will also left to return to their table.

Watching Eileen walk away, Bess said, "We have to do something. This is more serious than I thought."

"What's the problem?" Tim asked.

Kara filled him in. "Maybe you guys can help us think of someone we can get for a date for Eileen. We've run into a roadblock here."

"Last time I checked, Wilder's male population was every bit as big as Wilder's female population," Tim said. "I don't see what's so hard about finding her a date."

Bess shook her head and grinned. "You don't get it. Eileen's requirements are a bit more than just 'must be male.' He has to be a particular specimen of male."

"Huh?" Tim asked, looking confused. "Like what?"

"For one thing, he's got to be tall," Liz said.

"But not too tall," Casey added.

"Tall, but not too tall," Tim said, nodding.

"He's got to be artistic and sensitive," Bess chimed in.

Liz cut in. "But not a wimp either."

Bess saw Tim look over at Daniel and raise an eyebrow. "And he's got to be athletic but not muscle-bound," she said.

"Very intelligent and fun-loving," Casey said.

"Someone she can intellectually bond with," Kara added.

Before long, every woman at the table had had a turn. They eagerly contradicted one another and laughed as they assembled their friend's dream guy.

"And he's got to have a really cool car," Stephanie supplied.

Bess rolled her eyes in Stephanie's direction. "I don't think Eileen would care about the kind of car he drives."

Tim and Daniel shook their heads. Tim spoke loudly. "Fine. Forget the car. We think we know the kind of guy Eileen wants—if she doesn't mind a guy with three heads and four personalities."

"Well, you asked, and we told you," Bess said. "But if the job's too big for you we'll find someone else who can handle it."

"Just leave it to a couple of Alpha men," Tim joked.

As the night drifted on, Bess suddenly realized who might be able to find the perfect guy for Eileen.

Of course, why didn't I think of him before—Paul Cody, Bess thought to herself. My boyfriend just might be up to the challenge.

Casey began to feel cramped in the crowded room, and she stood up, slowly making her way over to where George and Will were sitting.

"Hey," she said. "I haven't gotten a chance to talk with you two in a while. How's it going?"

"Just fine," George said. "The Beat Poets sound good tonight."

Casey nodded. "I agree. Although I have to admit I've been so caught up in 'Project Find a Dream Guy for Eileen' that I haven't been paying all that much attention."

"Guess you'll have to buy the CD," Will replied.

George leaned forward. "I couldn't hear what was happening. What do you mean, find a dream guy for Eileen?" she asked.

Casey laughed and explained what they'd been talking about. "So what do you think?"

George laughed. "I'm all for it. I just hope one way or another you all turn up a guy as perfect for Eileen as Will is for me, and Charley is for you."

"And speaking of Charley," Will cut in, "I never did get a chance to say congratulations to you on your engagement. I guess we'll be calling you Mrs. Stern sometime soon."

"Well, thanks," Casey said. "I'm pretty excited about the whole thing. It's a great feeling to have things settled, but you won't be calling me Mrs. Stern for quite a while. Since we're waiting until I graduate to get married, it'll be a long engagement."

She took a sip of her drink and twirled the straw around in her glass. As she did so, she thought about Charley.

Before coming to Wilder, Casey had been a teen TV star with her own show, called *The President's Daughter*. She'd met Charley when he was cast as her boyfriend on the show, and they'd fallen in love. Then Casey decided she wanted to experience a normal life, and had left the show and Hollywood to attend Wilder.

Their romance continued, long-distance, until Charley had shown up a few weeks ago with a proposal of marriage. After much discussion, they'd finally agreed to wait to marry until Casey graduated in four years.

Her eyes traveled to the sparkling diamond on her left hand. Okay, so it was pretty big. Almost embarrassingly so. But it was a Hollywood thing. Everything larger than life.

And although she might be putting her career temporarily on hold, Casey wasn't too far removed from that world. Actually, she'd just heard the news that a little bit of Hollywood was coming to Wilder University.

"Sean Fletcher," she said under her breath. She tried to tell herself that she was every bit as excited to see Erika Swann, who'd once guest-starred on *The President's Daughter.*

Who am I kidding, she thought. It was Sean who excited her the most. She'd met him a few times, and she'd never forgotten how devastatingly handsome he was.

What do you care, she chided herself. You're engaged, remember?

So what? It wasn't as if she was planning to do anything about it. After all, she was wearing a ring—and Charley Stern was every bit as handsome as Sean.

It's a relief not to have to deal with the dating scene, right? Casey smiled and nodded firmly as if to convince herself.

*   *   *

Paul Cody turned up the front walk of the Zeta house and wearily shifted the weight of his heavy backpack. Pausing for a moment, he took a deep lungful of cool evening air. He'd spent the last several hours studying for exams, and now the cheerful laid-back atmosphere of his fraternity house beckoned.

"Hey, Cody, a couple of us are going to play pool," called one of his fraternity brothers as Paul stepped inside and crossed the front room toward the stairs. "Want to join us?"

"Some other time," Paul said. Normally, he'd be up for pool, but right then it didn't appeal to him. He was bleary eyed, and he just wanted to give his brain a well-deserved rest.

"Turning into a schoolboy on us, are you, Cody?" teased one of the guys, who was noted for being one of the biggest slackers in the house.

"Yeah, I guess I am," Paul said lightly and headed upstairs to his room. As he opened the door, he heard the shrill ring of his phone.

"Hey, Bess," he said, after picking up the receiver and hearing the sound of her voice. He dumped his backpack and sat on his bed. "This is a nice surprise. What's up?"

"Not much," Bess replied. "How's the studying going?"

"Oh, well enough. I'll be glad when exams are behind us, and we can get back to our usual stressload," he said cheerfully. "Are you making any headway?"

"Yes," Bess answered. "But that's not what I was calling about. I have an important question for you."

"Lay it on me," Paul said, happy to hear from her no matter what the reason. I love listening to the sound of her voice, he thought, sitting back with his long blue-jean-clad legs stretched out in front of him.

"I have a problem," Bess began. "Okay, so it's not a big one, and maybe it's not exactly mine—"

"Bess," Paul interrupted, laughing. "Just spit it out."

"It's Eileen," Bess said. "I've got to find her a date for the Alpha Delt formal. And it's not as easy as it seems. She's pretty particular. He's got to be a cut above the average guy. You know, good-looking, athletic but sensitive, but not muscle-bound."

Paul laughed. "Oh, so is that all the use you have for me?" he joked. "Paul Cody, date finder."

"Of course you know it's not." Bess laughed. "But this is important. Do you know anyone?"

Paul scanned his wall as if an answer might be there. "Okay, you got me," he said. "Eileen is a nice girl and all, but if she's as particular as you say she is, I don't know."

"Paul, I wouldn't ask, except that it's important," Bess said.

"I'm thinking, I'm thinking," Paul said. He picked up a paper airplane someone had left lying on his desk and sent it on a trajectory toward the door. Just as the plane hit the door, it was thrown open. Paul's towering roommate, Emmet Lehman, stepped in. He was still wearing his Wilder Norsemen football jacket but had on a white shirt and neat crewneck sweater under it.

"Paul," Bess said. "You still there?"

Paul stared at Emmet for a moment while he cradled the receiver in his hand. An idea was beginning to penetrate his study-numbed brain. Wilder women had been attracted to Emmet since the day he'd set foot on campus. But he was still single even though he'd broken up with his girlfriend over the summer. What was more, Emmet had been slaving over a killer paper. There was no doubt in Paul's mind that he'd be up for some fun in his life.

"Paul? Paul?" Bess's voice sounded faraway.

Suddenly Paul smiled, and he put the phone back to his ear again.

"Bess, I think I just found the answer to Eileen's dilemma," he said. "Your worries are over."

CHAPTER 3

George sipped the strong espresso from one of Will's chipped blue mugs and smiled as she listened to his off-key warble coming from the shower. The morning sun spilled in through the small window over the sink. She loved sitting in Will's apartment. It felt so peaceful.

"Oh, thank goodness, it's Friday," George thought happily. It had been a long week. Okay, so maybe the weekend would be more of the same—jam-packed with studying—but at least there wouldn't be classes, and her schedule wouldn't be so tight. She was mentally reviewing her study strategy when the phone rang and she answered it.

"Hi, George." It was Pam. "Remember me? I was your roommate in a former life. Long time no see. Just called to let you know that someone named Marta from your Western civ class phoned you. She wants you to call back

29

as soon as you can. She didn't leave a number."

"Thanks," George said. "I'll call her. I think I scrawled her phone number on my notebook somewhere. So what's going on with you? Are you buried under exams?"

George heard Pam's light laugh over the phone line. "I'll say."

George suddenly realized that she hadn't seen Pam in several days and was eager to know what was going on with her. "So what else is happening?"

"Oh, the usual. Studies. Work," Pam said. "Hey, one thing I haven't told you. Guess who I ran into at Berrigan's?" Without pausing she went on. "Stephanie. She's got a job there now. She started employee training, and she looks anything but happy about it."

"Probably the first bit of work she's ever done in her entire life," George said.

"She wouldn't even acknowledge me. She looked through me as if I was something bad that she'd stepped in," Pam said.

"That's Stephanie," George replied.

They talked for several minutes before Pam announced that she had to get ready for a class. "Talk to you soon," she said. "Are you ever coming home again? You spend so much time at Will's apartment, you might as well get married and make it official," she joked.

"Very funny," George said. But after she

hung up, she sat very still as Pam's words echoed in her mind. Suddenly she didn't feel as cheery as she had earlier.

Eileen O'Connor jostled her way through the crowd at the Copacetic Carrot, her eyes searching the crowded health-food co-op.

"Over here, Eileen," called Bess. She, Liz, and Kara were seated at a table by the cash register.

As she walked over to the table, Eileen felt her suspicions mount. Bess's call that morning had awakened her. And when Bess had told Eileen that she simply had to meet her for lunch, she hadn't mentioned why. Or that she'd be inviting anyone else.

"All right, you guys, what's going on here?" Eileen asked, deciding to get right to it. She sat down on the hard seat next to Liz.

"Nothing," Liz said too brightly.

Neither Liz's statement nor Kara's wide-eyed look of innocence could fool Eileen. It was clear that they were up to something. Was it her imagination, or did Bess look extremely guilty? Eileen was about to ask again when the young waitress came over to their table.

"We found you a date for the party," Bess announced after the waitress had taken their orders for salads and juice.

Eileen felt a warm flush creep up her cheeks as she took in Bess, who looked as if she was expecting a medal at the least. This I don't need, Eileen grumbled to herself.

"Thanks for your interest, but I made it plain before that I'm not in the market for a date for the party."

"But he's perfect," Liz said.

"No way," Eileen said flatly. "I don't want a date, and anyway I already have plans for that night."

Bess smiled in a way that got under Eileen's skin. A sort of I-know-what's-best-for-you smile. "That's right. You've got a date for dinner and dancing with Mr. Absolutely Perfect."

Even Eileen had to laugh, and she could see that Bess took it as a sign that she was beginning to crack. The waitress appeared with the juice part of their order.

"His name is Emmet Lehman, and he's Paul's roommate." Bess's words tumbled over each other after the waitress left. "You might have seen him at the Black and White Nights event. Anyway, he's nice looking, and big, as in football player big. Sandy blond hair. Ring a bell?"

"I don't remember anyone like that from the fund-raiser party," Eileen said. "As I said before, thanks, but no thanks."

"Eileen, I won't let you miss an opportunity you might regret for the rest of your life," Bess said, fixing her with an overly dramatic stare.

Eileen cracked a smile and scanned the faces

of her friends. It was clear that they weren't about to let up.

Finally she put up a hand. "Okay, okay, I give up. I surrender," she said. "Even if it's a total nightmare date, it's better than having you three haranguing me nonstop. Anything so you'll shut up and leave me alone."

Bess sipped her juice. "I knew you'd see reason," she said in a satisfied tone, just as the waitress appeared with their salads.

Casey took a seat next to Nancy in a middle row of Hewlitt's screening room. Casey hadn't expected anyone she knew to be at the screening, but when she'd gone back to Thayer Hall to get dressed, she was surprised to learn that Nancy was going, too. They'd decided to go together.

"Whoa. Check this out. We should have gotten here earlier," Casey said, glancing around the rapidly filling room. "This place is jammed. I had no idea how popular this film was going to be."

Nancy nodded. "Neither did I. Now, why do I get the distinct feeling that we are majorly underdressed?" she murmured, looking down at her black leggings and white tunic.

"We're not underdressed exactly. More like we're about thirty years ahead of our time," Casey said with a little laugh. "Check out the props people are carrying. Why is that guy lugging around a tire iron?"

"Jake told me about the *Road to Nowhere* cult following. He said a lot of fans have made the screenings of the movie into a circus, but I had no idea what to expect. This is unbelievable," Nancy said as she turned and looked around. She pointed to a group of girls entering the back door of the theater.

"Hey, there's Kara just coming in. I didn't know she was part of this craziness."

"Oh my gosh, they're all wearing hot pink micro minis like the one the lead character wears in the movie," Casey said, taking in Kara and a couple of her Pi Phi sisters, Montana Smith and Nikki Bennett. When they spotted Nancy and Casey, they maneuvered through the high-spirited crowd to make their way down to the empty seats directly behind them.

"I've already seen a bunch of other people wearing hot pink minis just like those," Nancy said. "I wondered what the significance was." She jerked her head toward a group of people wearing patched denim jeans and jackets. "Wow, check out those clothes!"

"To think I wasted time studying when I could have been designing my wardrobe," Casey said with a laugh.

Kara and her friends finally managed to squeeze in behind them. "Whew, we finally made it. Isn't this exciting?" Kara's eyes were sparkling.

"It's great," Nancy said. "I wish I'd dressed for the occasion."

Kara smiled. "We've been planning this for days. A lot of my Pi Phi sisters love *Road to Nowhere*. We scrounged up these outfits to look just like the ones in the movie. And check out my necklace. It's almost like the real thing. I made it myself."

Casey and Nancy looked closer at a pendant hanging on a black leather thong that Kara was wearing.

"Total flashback," Nancy said. "Next screening, I'll consult you about what to wear."

Kara nodded. "Good. I didn't want to tell you, but we almost didn't sit near you. You 'nongroovy chicks' just aren't with it," she joked.

Nikki leaned forward. "Guess what? We got a glimpse of Erika Swann. Wow. Talk about glamorous!" she exclaimed, batting eyelashes that were heavily coated with thick mascara. "Do you think she dyes her hair to get it to be so black?"

"I think Erika looks beautiful," Casey replied. "Hey, have you seen Sean Fletcher anywhere?" She was craning her neck, trying to look out over the crowd to see if she could spot him.

Montana shook her head. "If I had, I'd be

asking him for his autograph right now, not sitting here with you."

Just then a tall guy walked onto the stage in front of the movie screen. He was wearing patched jeans and carrying a small mike. He held up two fingers in a peace sign to quiet the crowd.

"I'm Terry Schneider, for those of you who don't know me, and I'm going to be brief here," he said. "Welcome to the Focus Film Society's Sebastian Fletcher Mini Film Festival. We're going to have some exciting things happening tonight. So sit back, enjoy *Road to Nowhere,* and afterward we've got some very special guests."

The lights dimmed, and the crowd whistled and cheered as *Road to Nowhere* started rolling. The audience members stood up and danced and sang along with the driving rock theme song.

> "Lead on, Road to Nowhere,
> Take me where you will,
> I ain't got nowhere better to go
> My torment won't be still. . . ."

"I can't believe everyone knows all the words," Casey whispered to Nancy.

"Neither can I," Nancy whispered back.

The movie opened with a surrealistic street scene. A thin, beautiful woman ran down an alleyway, her face contorted with sadness. She stepped in front of a bus, but at the last minute, it swerved and missed her. The woman collapsed in a heap at the side of the road, sobbing.

"Doesn't anyone hear?" she cried piteously.

"Doesn't anyone see?" the audience called back in unison with a swarthy man who stepped out of the shadows and knelt by the woman.

"Do these people have the entire dialogue memorized, too?" Nancy whispered as the audience continued to chime in at all the big moments.

"I guess so." Casey nudged Nancy. "Check out that hot pink micro mini that Erika Swann's character is wearing," she whispered. "Look familiar?"

By the final scene, the entire audience was on its feet, clapping and singing along with the closing song. Several people held up lighters and flames flickered in the dark. Then the lights came on, and Terry walked onto the stage again.

"Hope everyone enjoyed *Road to Nowhere*," he said.

The audience wolf-whistled and stomped appreciatively.

"I'd like to introduce a few of the people who contributed their artistry to the making of this film," Terry went on. He held out his hand as a tall, beautiful woman with jet black hair swept onto the stage. She was wearing a deep purple cape, which she swirled as she waved to the wildly clapping audience. She was followed by two men wearing jeans and black turtlenecks. "Meet Erika Swann, who played Kate Morelli. And this is Robert Delucca, the art director. And I'm sure you all recognize Sean Fletcher."

The clapping intensified.

"Erika Swann is so beautiful," Nancy whispered. "She's in amazing shape for someone in her fifties."

Casey nodded. "She was great to work with on my TV show. A little quirky at times but a very nice person."

The three film professionals sat in chairs up on the stage and began discussing the filming of *Road to Nowhere.*

"It rained a lot during production," Erika recalled. "There were constant delays. The cast got pretty antsy with all the retakes and uncertainties."

As Casey listened to the group talk, her thoughts drifted back to her filming days. She remembered the delays sometimes on the set of *The President's Daughter.* It had been stressful at times but still fun and exciting to step onto the set with the dazzling lights and the cameras rolling. Even now, she could still picture herself in her role.

But, Casey admitted, it hadn't all been glamour and good times. Sometimes people in the cast had squabbled. And then there were the tabloids. They were very capable at coming up with fictitious quarrels and other untrue stories about the cast members of *The President's Daughter.*

As Casey looked around her at the comforting familiarity of the Wilder auditorium, she smiled. No, she decided firmly, she didn't miss the film or TV world. University life was just fine for now.

Soon Terry opened up the discussion to the audience.

"Tell us about the scandal," someone called out. "About David Jacobs."

Casey leaned forward. She'd heard about this when she was out in Hollywood. The producer of *Road to Nowhere,* David Jacobs, had apparently committed suicide on the last day of filming. But the buzz around the film world had been that maybe it wasn't a suicide. No one was sure of the details, but Casey herself had heard numerous theories about Jacobs's death, and most of them had something to do with murder.

The theory she'd heard most often was that Lauren Fletcher, Sebastian's wife and Sean's mother, had had a scorching affair with Jacobs. The affair had ended during the filming of *Road to Nowhere.* The rumor was that Jacobs had been the one to break off the affair, and that Lauren, brokenhearted and distraught, had killed Jacobs and made it appear to be a suicide.

It was clear to Casey that Erika and Robert Delucca were caught off guard by the question. They looked uncomfortable as Terry stepped forward. "I don't think that's really an appropriate question to ask our guests at this time," he started, but was waved off by Sean.

"No, it's okay," he said.

Casey was surprised. After all, this tragedy did involve his father and mother.

"I don't mind talking about it," Sean said. "The police never did officially classify the death as a suicide. The investigation is still open, but I hope to find some resolution and put an end to the rumors that cling to my mother still. I don't believe she did it."

He went on to explain about his parents' divorce shortly after Jacobs's death.

"I was a baby when it all happened, so what I know is pretty much what people told me," Sean said. "My mom left Hollywood, and everyone lost contact with her after a few months. I was raised by my dad with the help of housekeepers. I didn't really think about what my life would have been like with a mother until I was a little older. Then I began to think about it a lot.

"But it wasn't until recently that I tried to locate her. Tracked her as far as Chicago, but

I haven't been able to get any information about her there."

Poor Sean, Casey thought, moved by his sad story. Is that why he's such a good comedic actor? They say in Hollywood that comedians often have sad lives. They turn to making other people laugh in order not to feel their own pain. Losing his mother at such a young age must have been so painful for Sean. Making audiences laugh probably helps him find happiness now.

Nancy was riveted to the discussion swirling around her. It seemed to her that there was more drama behind the scenes than in the film itself! And the film hadn't lacked for drama either.

"What a life he's had," Nancy said to Casey. "I used to think he had it made, I mean, being a big movie star and the son of a famous director and all. I had no idea."

After Sean finished, Robert Delucca stood up and held up several boards with distinctive necklaces and bracelets mounted on them. A couple of the film society members rolled in a case carrying a mannequin with one of the costumes worn by Lauren Fletcher.

"I've brought a bit of the original jewelry from the film. The costume department at the studio still had it stored away," he said. "From what I heard out there in the audience, I think some of you might recognize a few of these."

He paused as the audience laughed. Many of the young women were wearing replicas of the jewelry.

"I'm sorry I wasn't able to bring more, but many of the props and costumes have been lost over the years," DeLucca explained.

At the end of his discussion, he passed out souvenir publicity photos of the last scene in the movie showing all of the principal characters.

"Wow," Kara said, holding hers. "Great photo. But I'm bummed. I wish he'd brought the necklace that Erika's character wore. I wanted to see how close I came." She pointed to her own homemade version.

Nancy compared Kara's necklace to that in the photo she was holding. Erika's necklace had a detailed pendant hanging from it. Kara's was a cruder version.

"I do have something special to share with you," Sean said after DeLucca sat down. "It's not commonly known, but Sebastian had considered a different ending to *Road to Nowhere.* He had even shot an alternate final scene. But after Jacobs's death, he changed his mind. I've brought the reel of the alternate ending. It's never been shown before, and I'd like you to see it. And I've even got a reel of outtakes. It seems there's quite a collection of flubbed lines. I hope you'll find them as funny as I did."

The audience applauded wildly and Nancy settled back to enjoy the unexpected treat. But as she waited for Terry to slip in the new reel, she found herself drawn into thinking about Sean and the scandal surrounding his parents. What an amazing story, she thought. And though the mystery surrounding Jacobs's death was definitely intriguing, Nancy realized that she was more interested in Sean's story of trying to find his mother. After all, she knew what it was like to grow up without a mother. Her own mother had died when she was three.

"Poor Sean," Nancy murmured to herself. "I hope he doesn't give up searching for his mother. I'm sure she's out there— somewhere."

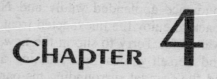

CHAPTER 4

Unbelievable! We did it!" Bess said, slamming closed her textbook and reaching over to hug Paul. The two of them were sprawled on the floor in Bess's room, surrounded by a sea of books and papers. "An entire evening spent studying without an interruption."

Paul nodded and pushed back a lock of thick golden hair that had fallen forward on his forehead. "A definite landmark event. I mean, there you were, providing me with incredible distraction, and yet I was able to concentrate on my book."

He leaned over for a closer look at Bess's thick biology text. "Wow. You finished three chapters. I think you set a record for yourself."

"I think I did, too," Bess said. She reached up and traced one of Paul's laugh lines which framed his beautiful eyes. Suddenly her stomach growled.

"I can't believe it. We forgot to eat. I think it's time for the victory feast. Should we go mad, throw caution to the wind, and take some time out from studying?"

"Sounds perfect to me," Paul said with a laugh. "I could use a Pizza Truck offering about now."

"I'm all for pizza," Bess said. "But the Pizza Truck? My friends and I searched for it forever the other night. Don't you think it's possible we might starve to death before we find it?"

Paul grinned. "It's a definite risk. But food always tastes better when you have to hunt it down."

Sighing, Bess stood up and stretched. "I guess you're right. It's all part of the fun."

She pulled on her Wilder sweatshirt, and she and Paul set out in search of the truck. First, they walked toward the quad and made a sweep past the library.

"I'm fading," Bess moaned.

Paul made a great show of sniffing the air. "Never fear. My pepperoni radar has never let me down yet. Let's try over by Graves Hall."

Bess slogged on, listening to her stomach growl louder and louder. But no luck. Finally, just as she was about to persuade Paul to give up and head to the Hot Truck, which they'd seen near the library, for a sandwich instead, Bess spotted it in the parking lot by the Student Union.

"There it is, there it is!" she shouted.

"Popular place tonight," Paul observed as they neared the truck and its long line. "Looks like a lot of people had the same idea we did."

"Pepperoni on the brain," Bess said happily as she and Paul joined the line. Now that she was in no danger of starving, Bess felt particularly pleased with herself for the amount of studying she had accomplished, in spite of a huge distraction in the form of Paul Cody. There had been a time in the not-too-distant past when Bess had wondered if she'd ever get the hang of studying. And now look at her!

"Hi, Bess," called Leslie King, Bess's roommate. She and her newly acquired boyfriend, Nathan Kress, were standing in front of the order window. Leslie waved, and Bess lifted her hand to return the greeting.

It was unbelievable, Bess thought. Her uptight study-freak roommate had finally looked up from her books long enough to fall head over heels in love with Nathan. And what a difference falling in love had made for Leslie. Almost overnight, she'd gone from being a bristly, critical person to a softer, more relaxed one. Talk about a transformation!

"Hi, Leslie. Hi, Nathan," Bess called out. "Taking a study break, too?"

Leslie shook her head, so that her long hair rippled softly against her shoulders. "No," she said.

Get a clue, Bess, she thought to herself. Leslie definitely wasn't wearing study clothes. Instead, she was wearing a soft, fuzzy pink sweater, and white pants under her open coat. In the garish light from the Pizza Truck, Bess could see that Leslie was even wearing makeup.

"Actually, Nathan and I were at the movies," Leslie went on. "We just saw a great film. Funny, and definitely romantic." She snuggled closer to Nathan and grinned.

Bess tried not to show her surprise. Her roommate was a premed student, and she had been one of the biggest grinds on campus. It wasn't like her to blow off a study opportunity to go to the movies, especially to see a lightweight romantic comedy.

Leslie lowered her voice. "Actually, if the truth be known, I've barely cracked a book all week."

"Oh," Bess said. She took another look at her roommate, then over at Nathan. He slipped one arm around Leslie and dropped a kiss onto her head.

Leslie smiled and turned away from Bess. It was obvious they were totally crazy about each other. But the thought crossed Bess's mind that maybe they were taking their studies a little too casually.

I mean, even Paul and I managed to study, and we're doing a pretty good job of putting together a relationship, Bess thought.

I ought to say something to Leslie, Bess decided. But after taking a look at the way Leslie was super-glued to Nathan, she decided not to. Leslie looked so dreamy and happy that Bess didn't have the heart.

Still, Bess thought, turning back to look at the pizza topping selections, Leslie had better not waste too much time goofing off. She might be smart, but everyone knew that it took more than mere brain power to survive premed courses at Wilder. It took hours and hours of major studying as well.

The next minute Bess chuckled lightly. Imagine, her, Bess Marvin, wanting to lecture someone like Leslie about studying!

"It never occurred to me before that films could have endings different from the ones shown in theaters," Nancy said to Casey as they walked back to Thayer Hall.

"You'd be surprised how often it happens," Casey said. "Of course, most of the time, the alternate endings are stored and no one ever gets the chance to view them. We were lucky to see this one."

"Just think, if they'd released the alternate ending, *Road to Nowhere* would have ended up being a very different film," Nancy replied. "I have to tell you, though, that I liked the original ending best."

"So did I," Casey agreed. "There was something about that alternate ending that just didn't fit. I can't quite put my finger on it."

"I know what you mean," Nancy said. "I had a feeling that something was slightly off. And what's amazing to me is that someone put a lot of work into it. All for something that ended up getting set aside and stored away for years."

"I used to think about some of the footage of the different shows for *The President's Daughter*," Casey mused. "We'd shoot scenes hour after hour. Sometimes, we'd film several different scenarios. And in the end, we had only a twenty-minute segment, plus commercials, to show for all those hours we'd put in."

"It must have been frustrating," Nancy said.

"Oh, every once in a while it would get to me," Casey replied. "But it was just part of the job."

"There are a lot of technical aspects to film work I never even considered before," Nancy added. "For example, when they reshot the ending, they had to make sure everything still tied in smoothly to the rest of the work."

Casey nodded. "It's not easy to achieve that continuity. It takes a lot of attention to detail to make sure that things are consistent within each scene and setting. Props, costumes, actual spots where the characters stand. Things like that. Some people's entire jobs revolve around making sure things are seamless in filming."

"It's unreal," Nancy said. "I never really thought about all that before."

Casey laughed. "Good thing someone does. The *Road to Nowhere* crew obviously was very professional. Sebastian Fletcher was known for being a meticulous director. But I've seen some grade B gems that were filled with glitches you wouldn't believe. They're pretty hysterical."

"Too bad we ran out of time to see that outtake reel," Nancy said. "I was looking forward to it. I guess we all got so caught up in the discussion, we didn't realize how late it was."

"Well, we don't have to wait that long to see the outtakes," Casey said as they walked into the dorm. "Didn't Terry say that they'd show them the last day of the festival?"

Nancy nodded and pressed the elevator button in the lobby of Thayer Hall. When they reached Suite 301, Nancy fumbled for her keys, and they let themselves in.

Stephanie was sitting on the sofa in the lounge with one of her long legs draped over the armrest in a studied, casual pose.

"Oh, hi there," she drawled as she took a deep drag on her cigarette. Smoke curled lazily around her head. "I know, I know. Too much smoke in here. But, hey, I was the only one in."

Nancy didn't feel like getting into it with Stephanie, so she didn't say anything.

Stephanie took another drag. "Big night at the movies?" she asked.

"Well, yes," Nancy said. "It was pretty exciting. We saw a screening of *Road to Nowhere*. One of the stars was there and"—Nancy stopped when she saw that Stephanie wasn't listening. She was looking moodily at the darkened TV screen in front of her.

Why do I bother, Nancy thought. She was about to walk on, but something in Stephanie's expression stopped her. "Everything okay?"

Stephanie's laugh was hollow. "About as okay as can be expected."

"What does that mean?" Casey asked.

Nancy knew that Stephanie probably wouldn't answer, so she was surprised when Stephanie said, "Pull up a sofa, and I'll tell you my sad story."

Nancy exchanged glances with Casey, and they sat down. Stephanie stubbed out her cigarette in an empty soda can.

"I start my new job tomorrow. Stephanie Keats, sales dog. Has a nice ring doesn't it?" she said sarcastically.

She paused, then went on. "Employee training was the worst. The supervisors treated us like morons. They made us read these stupid manuals and role play. I'm going to hate every single minute working at Berrigan's."

"I know someone who works there—Pam Miller," Nancy said. "Pam doesn't mind. She says the hours are pretty flexible so that she can work around her classes and social life."

"Humph," Stephanie muttered. "It's outrageous that I have to work. I've never worked in my life. It's so degrading."

"Oh, cheer up. It won't be that bad," Casey said soothingly. "If things get out of hand, just pretend you're acting, that you're playing a part in a movie or something."

Stephanie smiled wryly. "Leave it to an actress to tell me how to act my way out of a problem. But I might take your advice. If you want to know the truth, I think my whole life is like a bad movie!"

"Hi, guys. How goes the computer business these days?" George asked as she maneuvered into the small booth next to Will. She smiled at Reva Ross and her boyfriend, Andy Rodriguez, who were seated across from them, studying their menus.

"Busy as ever," Reva said. "But right now, I'm much more interested in what to eat."

"Their chili burgers are the best," Andy said.

"Definitely," George agreed. She took a menu and glanced idly at it. She really wasn't in the mood to be here, and she wished Will hadn't promised to meet Reva and Andy tonight. It was weird, she thought. Ordinarily, she looked forward to dinner out with her friends. Now all she felt like doing was heading for her cozy dorm room and being by herself.

After the waiter took their orders, Reva spoke up.

"Guess what?" she said, excitement dancing in her large dark eyes. "Andy and I just started working on a Web site for Wilder."

"That's great!" George exclaimed. She hated to admit it, but she wasn't sure exactly what that would mean to a university.

"Of course, it's all in the beginning stages, but one day the school can use the site to give out information on admissions and new programs and who knows what else," Andy said.

"Good going," Will said. "There's no end to what you guys can do on the computer."

Reva grinned. "We've got to stay one step ahead of the techno game. That's what it's all about."

Soon the waiter brought their food, and the conversation drifted from computers to classes. George found herself pulling back from the conversation and studying Will and her friends while they talked. It was all so familiar—the chili burgers, the conversation, the way Will sometimes finished her sentences for her when he knew what she was going to say next.

Funny, George thought, staring into the diner windows at her reflection, anyone looking at them would think they'd been together forever. A stranger walking in could easily mistake her and Will for a married couple having dinner with another couple.

"Thank goodness it's Friday, as they say. I need a weekend, that's for sure. I think I fried my brain from all the studying I've been doing," Reva's voice drifted into George's thoughts.

"Tell me about it," Will said. "I'm even studying in my dreams. The other night, I dreamed for hours about endless papers I was writing. Is that sick or what?"

"Definitely," Andy agreed. "It's kind of contagious these days. I haven't met too many people who are immune."

"George, wing me the dessert menu, will you?" Reva asked, leaning past Andy so she could be heard.

"Hey, George, you still with us?" Will said loudly in her ear.

It suddenly registered that her friends were talking to her. "Sorry," George said. "What did you want? I wasn't paying attention."

"The dessert menu, please," Reva repeated.

"We're hurt. Our conversation wasn't riveting?" Andy teased.

George passed the menu and looked around at everyone. Then she smiled apologetically. "No, you were absolutely riveting as always," she said. "It's just me, out to lunch when I should be out to dinner with you guys."

Will put an arm around her shoulder and gave her an affectionate squeeze. "Exams on your mind?"

No, George thought, but she nodded. Actually, Will was probably the last person that she could tell about what was on her mind. For some reason, after Pam's comment on the phone that morning about being married, the subject of marriage was all George could think about.

Sitting there, feeling the warmth of his hand on her shoulder, George was aware of the current that flowed between them. She could imagine herself being with him forever. Having a home together, sharing in all kinds of adventures, traveling all over the world, and growing old together.

But then as she studied Will's lean, coppery profile, another thought crept into her brain. Of course, it wouldn't all be easy. After all, keeping a marriage together through the pressures of school and beyond would take a lot of work. But, she told herself firmly, she and Will had already been through some tough times. They would survive anything they ran up against in the future. Their love was strong.

In some ways, George reflected, she felt so mature, but when she really looked at it, she realized that she was still so young. Too young to settle down with one guy. She should be testing her wings and having fun learning about all the other guys out there. She shook her head as if to rid herself of the thought. Unthinkable to imagine herself with anyone but Will. But marriage was too serious to consider at this stage in her life.

As the evening wore on, George felt herself even more removed from her surroundings. She had trouble paying attention to what was going on around her, and she had to force herself to respond whenever someone asked her a question. It was getting tiring keeping a smile pasted on her face. She just wasn't in the mood for laughter and light bantering. When Reva mentioned ordering coffee, George stood up.

"Sorry to spoil the fun," she said with a yawn, "but I'm beat."

She didn't meet Will's eyes when they turned to her.

After George and Will said good night to Reva and Andy, they strolled toward the parking lot.

"You okay?" Will asked. "You didn't talk much tonight."

George nodded. "Just tired," she mumbled.

Will studied her face, then turned to unlock his motorcycle. George hopped on the back of the bike, and they roared off into the night. The cool night air contrasted sharply with the warmth of Will's back. George rested her cheek against his leather-jacketed shoulder and breathed deeply. Normally, Will's presence brought things sharply into focus for George. But tonight, it only served to confuse her further. As Will started automatically toward his apartment, George tapped him on the back of his helmet.

"Would you mind taking me back to Jamison instead?" she shouted.

Will called back, "Well, sure, I guess so."

"I—I just need to be alone tonight," George started to say. But there was no way she could explain. She tried to convince herself it was because the roar of the motorcycle cut off any conversation they might have had.

Chapter 5

"Here it is, Saturday morning," Stephanie muttered. "Everyone else is sleeping in, and I'm off to join the working drones of America."

She glanced at her reflection in the plate glass doors. Her tight dress set off her figure magnificently, she decided. It was the perfect shade of green.

She looked at the clock just inside the main door in Berrigan's. Two minutes until nine. Too early for work, as far as Stephanie was concerned. But Mrs. Caldwell had been clear.

"Report to the Studio Ten Department at nine A.M.," she'd said crisply to Stephanie the day before.

Walking slowly, Stephanie made her way to Studio 10, the department for older women's clothing.

"Well, now what?" she murmured, looking around her. She didn't see a supervisor or any

58

other salespeople. There weren't any customers. So what was she supposed to do?

After setting her purse in a cabinet under the cash register, Stephanie leaned against the counter and studied the gaudy clothing displayed on the racks.

This stuff is dee-pressing, Stephanie thought. Remind me to drop dead before I get so old that I think burnt orange looks good. Suddenly she had a thought. Maybe she'd use her employee discount and buy her dear stepmother Kiki a birthday gift. Stephanie laughed out loud at the thought of Kiki wearing a bright orange sack.

"I got it just for you," she'd say sweetly.

Am I supposed to stand around all day leaning on this counter with nothing to do? Stephanie thought with disgust. Talk about mind numbing. Maybe she'd sneak off somewhere and have a smoke. Just then an overly made-up woman with hair piled up like an explosion burst through an employee door and marched over to her.

"There you are. You must be the new girl. I was looking for you. I'm Mrs. Moreno, senior sales associate," the woman announced, peering at Stephanie's name tag. "You were supposed to come through the employee entrance."

"Was I?" Stephanie asked with a loud yawn.

"Yes. I'm sure Mrs. Caldwell made that perfectly clear to you during your training. You have to punch in your time card," Mrs. Moreno said. She looked Stephanie up and down.

"And let this be the last time I have to tell you this, Stephanie Keats. Sales personnel do not wear flimsy, skin tight clothing, and they are not to loll against the counters. If you can't find something to do, you are to make yourself busy. Go punch in, and when you come back, start refolding those sweaters on the table."

Stephanie's eyes traveled over to the display. "But they look perfectly fine to me."

"It doesn't matter," Mrs. Moreno snapped. "Get busy."

On her way to the time clock, Stephanie thought about Mrs. Moreno's poufy bluish hair and her ultra-tight face, which had been nipped and tucked in every way imaginable. How many face lifts have you had, you old bag, Stephanie wanted to ask. When she returned, she sauntered over to the sweaters and refolded them quickly, aware that Mrs. Moreno was watching her every move.

When Stephanie was almost finished, the senior salesperson came over to inspect her work. "This just won't do. The stacks are crooked, and some of the sleeves are hanging out. Start again."

"Yes, ma'am," Stephanie said, rolling her eyes. This time, she folded the sweaters more neatly, daring Mrs. Moreno to find fault. But Mrs. Moreno appeared to be satisfied.

"So now what?" Stephanie asked. "This place sure is dead. Don't you ever get any customers?"

"Oh, it'll be busy soon enough," the supervisor said, adding up a column of figures next to the cash register.

"Who picks the stuff for this department anyway?" Stephanie asked. "These clothes you stock must seriously scare people away."

"If that was meant to amuse me, it missed the mark," Mrs. Moreno said curtly. "Ah, here comes a customer now."

"I don't think she wants to be bothered," Stephanie said.

"All customers value our input," replied Mrs. Moreno. "Watch how I handle her. You just might learn something."

Stephanie deliberately turned her back and pretended to smooth some jackets hanging from a rack, but she could hear Mrs. Moreno's honeyed voice asking the woman if she'd seen the new line of sweaters that had just arrived. A few minutes later the woman was standing in front of a three-way mirror wearing one of the most hideous purple sweaters Stephanie had ever seen.

"Now, that looks as if it were made for you," gushed Mrs. Moreno. "See how it makes your eyes look violet."

"I think I'm going to hurl," Stephanie muttered to herself. "No way that woman will fall for that stupid line. She can see for herself she looks like an overripe grape in that rag."

But in no time it seemed, Mrs. Moreno was ringing up the sweater and a few other items, and the customer walked out with two large Berrigan's shopping bags.

"See how it's done?" Mrs. Moreno said smugly to Stephanie. "Here's another customer. Now you practice what you just learned about selling."

"Right," Stephanie said, and she moved toward a thin, nervous woman who was looking through the jackets Stephanie had just smoothed.

"Can I help you?" Stephanie said, trying to sound sweet.

The woman didn't look up from the rack. "No, thanks. Just looking."

"Whatever," Stephanie mumbled under her breath. She stepped back and tried to look busy. The customer slipped on a coral jacket and studied her reflection in the brightly lit mirror.

"Nope," Stephanie called loudly, shaking her head. "You can't wear coral. You've got that skin coloring that goes completely dead with that color."

"Oh, I guess you're right. It doesn't look good at all," the woman said, embarrassed as she saw that a couple of other customers were now staring at her. She quickly shrugged out of the jacket, rehung it, then walked out of the department.

"Don't ever let me hear you talk to a customer like that again," thundered Mrs. Moreno at Stephanie's elbow. "Look what you did."

Stephanie's head snapped up. "What are you talking about? Just because I was honest with her? Did you see how awful she looked?"

"We're in business to sell clothes, not to insult customers," Mrs. Moreno said, stalking off.

Stephanie set her jaw, then reached under the counter to grab her purse. She didn't know how much more of this she could take. She needed a cigarette now. With trembling fingers, she lit up a cigarette and was just about to inhale, when the cigarette was ripped right out of her mouth.

Mrs. Moreno put it out in the empty wastebasket and turned to Stephanie furiously.

"In case you haven't read the rules, which you were supposed to during your training session, Berrigan's has a strict no-smoking policy," she said. "Don't ever let me catch you smoking around here again."

"Sorry," Stephanie said.

What a battle-ax. Can this dump get any worse? Stephanie wondered as she waited on her next customer. This customer tried on at least six outfits and walked out without buying anything, earning Stephanie another icy look.

Oh, jeez, how long until coffee break? She was having a complete nic fit, and she didn't know how long she could go without killing someone.

Precisely at ten-thirty, Stephanie bolted toward the elevator bank. She'd go outside and light up, and even Mrs. Moreno couldn't say a word. She fidgeted as she waited for the elevator doors to open and when they did, she found herself face-to-face with one of the most gorgeous, well-dressed guys she'd ever seen.

Stephanie was immediately conscious of his gleaming chestnut brown hair. His slim but muscular build was set off by a magnificently tailored suit. He was wearing a Berrigan's logo pin on the lapel of his jacket. Stephanie gave him her biggest smile.

"Hi, I'm Stephanie Keats," she said brightly, preening so he'd get the full effect of her slinky dress. "I just started on the job today."

The guy mumbled something that passed for a hello, and as the door opened, he said, "Jonathan Baur," and walked out.

Not too talkative, Stephanie thought, pressing the button impatiently for the ground floor, but definitely cute.

Well, at least things were looking up a little if Jonathan Baur worked here. Now, Stephanie decided, if she could just find a decent place to smoke, maybe this job wouldn't be so bad after all.

*   *   *

"Good morning, Wilder ones. It's Saturday morning, and you're listening to Patrice's Personalities at Radio Wilder." The deejay's voice shot out from Bess's radio alarm, and she sat up to shut off the jarring sound.

As her head cleared, she looked around her dorm room. Leslie had already gotten up and was gone. But for the first time ever, her bed was unmade. Bess got up and stepped over several piles of Leslie's clothes. She chuckled a little.

This is a switch, she muttered to herself. Me, stepping over Leslie's mess.

The room was now a certified disaster, but at least Leslie was no longer on her case to keep it clean, Bess decided cheerfully. She started rooting through her things to find something to wear.

What was Leslie's blouse doing on her side of the room? Bess frowned as she tossed it over to Leslie's side. She rummaged on, trying to find her navy sweater. No luck. Sighing, she gave up and decided to settle for her red sweater. It too was nowhere to be found.

Bess stood up with her hands on her hips. This place was actually becoming kind of a pain to deal with, she thought. Even if Leslie was no longer carping about cleaning up, there was no doubt that things were definitely easier to find when at least *one* side of the room had been clean. With a sigh, Bess started picking up a few of her own things.

"How can you eat that? Isn't all that pepper hot?" Nancy asked in amazement as she watched her Helping Hands little sister, Anna Pederson, smother her pizza with red chili pepper flakes.

Nancy had joined the Helping Hands program, and been paired with Anna, a motherless twelve-year-old. The two spent time together every week, with Nancy filling a void that Anna's busy single father couldn't, by giving her a woman to talk to, shop with, go to movies, and out to eat with. Now they were sitting in a small pizzeria in Weston where Nancy had never been before.

"I like it this way," Anna said, her large brown eyes regarding Nancy. She took a huge bite of her slice.

Nancy sipped her soda and studied the young girl's worn clothing and thin face. Although Anna seemed content enough now that she had spent the morning with Nancy, Nancy hadn't missed the fact that Anna was quieter than usual. She had a feeling something was on Anna's mind.

I hope nothing is wrong, Nancy thought. Might as well take the direct approach, she decided. "Hey, Anna, you seem so quiet today. Is something bothering you?"

"Not really," Anna replied, a little too forced.

"Do you want to talk?" Nancy probed gently.

Anna shook her head and continued eating her pizza, stopping every so often to sprinkle on more red pepper flakes.

Something's going on, Nancy decided. But I'll have to be patient and let her tell me when she's ready. To break up the silence, Nancy found herself talking about the *Road to Nowhere* screening, highlighting a few of the more humorous scenes in the film.

When she mentioned that Sean Fletcher had been there, Anna lit up. Anna had once told her he was her favorite actor. Now she demanded that Nancy tell her everything about him and the other famous people she'd seen as well.

"Is Erika Swann as pretty as she was in those old movies?" Anna asked.

"Check it out for yourself," Nancy said, pulling out the publicity photo from her purse. "Look. I brought a photo for you to see. Here's Erika, and there's Lauren Fletcher. You might not know who she is, but she was a very good actress in her day."

"She's pretty. But why is everyone wearing such weird clothes?" Anna asked. "They look like geeks. And all that eye goop. Yuck!"

Nancy smiled. "That was the style in the sixties. People wanted to be different. At the screening last night, most of the people were dressed just like the characters in the movie. I never saw so many wild colors and so much bizarre jewelry. It was lots of fun."

Anna nodded. "Sounds like it. I used to like dressing up when I was a little kid."

"What do you like doing now? I mean besides shopping and eating pizza?" Nancy asked, eager to get to know her little sister better.

Anna shrugged. "Nothing much. Maybe looking at movie magazines."

When it came time to leave the restaurant, Nancy was glad to see that Anna definitely looked as if she was in a better frame of mind. As they walked toward Nancy's car, Anna chatted happily about movie stars. Suddenly she pointed at a long, elegant black limousine with tinted windows that was parked at the curb.

"That's Mrs. Vandenbrock's limo," Anna exclaimed. "Isn't it beautiful? When I grow up, I want a limo just like that."

Nancy's head snapped up at the mention of Mrs. Vandenbrock's name. She turned to look as the uniformed driver finished tightening the rear right wheel with a lug wrench. She was disappointed to notice that the windows were so dark she couldn't see inside. But just then, the window lowered a fraction, and Nancy could see the top of Mrs. Vandenbrock's head, an arresting set of blue eyes topped off by a distinctive widow's peak.

"Is that tire fixed yet, Baldwin?" the cool, silvery voice asked.

"Yes, madam," the driver responded.

Nancy wasted no time. She dashed over to the partially opened window.

"Good afternoon, Mrs. Vandenbrock," Nancy said hastily. "I'm Nancy Drew, and I interviewed you the other day. I was wondering if we could continue with the interview—"

"I'm afraid that won't be possible," Mrs. Vandenbrock said. "Good day." With that, she rolled up the window.

"But, Mrs. Vandenbrock—" Nancy sputtered.

The driver gave Nancy a measured look, and after dumping the flat tire in the trunk, climbed in the driver's seat. The limo slowly pulled away from the curb and snaked down the street. Nancy made her way back to Anna.

"Wow," Anna said, watching the limo. "Well, here's your photo back."

Nancy blinked, her mind still on the elusive Mrs. Vandenbrock, as she took the photo from Anna, and looked down at it.

Interesting, she thought suddenly. Mrs. Vandenbrock looks something like Lauren Fletcher. Same widow's peak and those gorgeous blue eyes. She sighed. It had been a great escape going to the movie screening and getting caught up in the fascinating scandal surrounding the filming. But Nancy reminded herself that she'd better tuck away the screen fantasy world and get real again. She still didn't have her profile piece for journalism class.

Well, Nancy decided, as soon as she dropped Anna off, she'd head to the Weston Public Library and try to get some information on Mrs. V. Maybe she'd get lucky and find some material on the woman and her husband. Then she might be able to write up a decent profile, even if she was thwarted in her attempts at a personal interview. She didn't want to think about what would happen if she didn't get the material she needed. After all, there just wasn't time to find a new person to interview for her assignment.

CHAPTER 6

Eileen pressed her forehead against her fingertips and looked outside at the afternoon sun. How long had she been cooped up in her room staring at textbooks, trying to cram facts and figures into her head? Too long! The whole morning had slipped away. It was time to get some blood pumping.

After changing into her gray cotton workout clothes, she headed out to the gym at the sports complex. A rigorous workout would be just what she needed.

"Good, it's not too crowded," Eileen said fifteen minutes later as she stepped into the workout room and took a look around. "And a free Nautilus machine."

As Eileen made her way over to it, a muscle-bound guy leaped in front of her and grabbed the machine.

"Do you mind?" Eileen said annoyed.

"What's your problem? I got here first," the guy said coldly.

"Yes, after you practically mowed me down," Eileen snapped.

"Maybe next time you'll be in better shape and be able to beat me out," the guy retorted. Then he turned away and started his workout.

Eileen glared at him. What an arrogant, self-centered jerk! she thought. She looked around the room and saw that the machine in the far corner had just been freed up. She started over toward it. No way was she going to let someone muscle in front of her again.

Eileen moved so quickly, she didn't watch where she was going. In the next second, she barreled into a tall, sandy-haired guy who cut across her path. Eileen ran up against him with such force that the wind was knocked out of her as she hurtled backward. Losing her balance, Eileen landed on the floor with a resounding *thwack*.

"I'm so sorry. Hey, you okay?" the guy said, the concern evident on his handsome face as he reached to help her up.

But Eileen was in no mood for concern that came a little too late. She shoved his hand away. Out of the corner of her eye, she saw the guy on the first Nautilus machine suppress a smile. This fueled her embarrassment and fury, which she unleashed on the man who'd just about knocked her cold. She glared at him and gasped out, "Nice going, you oversize clod."

The guy stepped back. "I said I was sorry. You don't have to get so heated about an accident."

Eileen stood up shakily. "Look, Mr. Steroid, you try keeping cool when you've just been slammed into by a freight train. Why don't you macho jock guys start watching where you're going around here?"

"I said I was sorry," the guy said in a clipped voice. "And why don't you put a lid on your rude attitude and accept people's apologies with a little grace. Jerk." With that, he stalked off.

Eileen shot him a venomous look. Her anger mounted. She was just too upset to try to work out now. Turning abruptly, she stormed out of the workout room.

Nancy shifted in the hard wooden seat in the library as she looked through the copies she'd made of the few newspaper articles on the Vandenbrock family. After spending a couple of hours scrolling through the microfilm, she hadn't made much headway. There just wasn't a lot of newspaper material.

First, she'd come across a short, after-the-fact wedding announcement. It stated simply that Wendell Vandenbrock married Leila Greer in Chicago in June of 1973. There was no accompanying photo. Setting aside this announcement, Nancy continued on. She looked at several mentions of cultural and charity events that the couple had attended. Then came Wendell's obituary in 1991. Very little information there. Nancy sighed.

"Ah-ha, now what have we here?" Nancy murmured as she glanced at a charity ball photo taken about ten years earlier, showing Mr. and Mrs. Vandenbrock. On a hunch, Nancy slipped out the *Road to Nowhere* publicity photo she'd carried in her backpack and laid it beside the newspaper photo. The newspaper picture wasn't very clear, but Nancy could feel herself starting to get excited. The photo was of a much younger Mrs. Vandenbrock, and in it she looked even more like Lauren Fletcher—those startling eyes and that distinctive widow's peak.

"Could it be?" Nancy whispered as she studied the photos.

She tried to tamp down her growing excitement as she considered the possibilities. Was this Sean's long-lost mother? Sean had mentioned tracking her as far as Chicago, but then he hadn't been able to find out anything further.

It did seem strange that Mrs. Vandenbrock didn't have much of a past, Nancy reflected. You'd think there'd be something about her before her marriage, a graduation announcement or some such thing. Then Nancy was struck by a thought. Maybe Leila Greer was a phony name. But why a phony name? Was Mrs. Vandenbrock hiding something?

Nancy set the photos down and sat staring at the ceiling, considering what to do next.

"I'll show the photos to Sean, and see what he makes of it all," she decided as she collected the copies and placed them in her backpack.

It was a long shot, but, Nancy thought, you just never know.

Tilting back on an overturned packing crate, Stephanie stretched out her long legs and took a deep drag of her cigarette. Okay, so maybe the loading dock of Berrigan's shipping department wasn't the most glamorous place to take a break. But as far as Stephanie was concerned, it would do just fine. For one thing, it sure beat going outside and freezing. And it hadn't taken Stephanie long to figure out that this was one place where she could smoke without being hassled.

"Hello, there," called a raspy, masculine voice.

Stephanie looked up as a delivery man walked by carrying several small boxes. He winked at her and stubbed out his own cigarette while waving away the telltale smoke.

Stephanie pointedly ignored him. She and

the delivery guys might share the common bond of having a smoke, but that didn't mean she was friends with them or anything.

As she smoked, Stephanie considered her plight. Wow, had her life changed drastically. From being able to buy almost anything she wanted, to having to work for every penny. Being a working girl was the worst thing that could have happened to her, she decided. It was so degrading.

"Look at me, sitting on a loading dock, dying of terminal boredom," she muttered. "And I have my dear stepmother to thank for this honor."

When Stephanie was finished, she stashed her cigarette butt under the crate and slipped out of the shipping area. She sure didn't want the witch who supervised the department to catch her. She'd already tangled with Mrs. Woodward a while ago when she'd run down an order. Stephanie had no doubt that Mrs. Woodward would love to jump down her throat if she caught her smoking in her area.

Stephanie was heading over to the cafeteria-style coffee shop located by the credit department when she bumped into Pam Miller. She looked around quickly, but there was no escape.

"Hello, Pam," Stephanie said without enthusiasm.

Pam grinned. "Stephanie. How's your first day on the job?"

Stephanie regarded Pam coolly. "Fine," she said noncommittally. "I hope the swill they serve at this coffee shop is at least semi-edible."

Pam shrugged. "I've been eating it for a few weeks, and it hasn't killed me yet. But I will warn you to stay away from the tuna salad. It's practically legend around here."

"Not to worry," muttered Stephanie, shuddering at the thought of sinking to eating tuna anything.

They took their place in line behind several other employees.

"Actually, if you want to know the truth, this whole work thing sucks," Stephanie said under her breath. "I think I've run into two contenders for the Witch of the Year title— my supervisor and the hag who heads up the shipping and order department."

"Oh, come on. The people are okay. You just have to get to know them," Pam said. "Do your work, and they'll leave you alone."

"That's all I've been trying to do," Stephanie grumbled as she took a wrapped turkey sandwich and inspected it suspiciously. "First Mrs. Moreno jumps all over my case for being honest with a customer, then she climbs all over me for entering my order numbers incorrectly. I mean, give me a break. It's my first day on the job. Does she expect perfection?"

Pam shook her head. "You'll get the hang of it around here. At least, the paycheck comes in handy. And if you get into a good department, like cosmetics, you get a bunch of free samples. So all in all, it's got some benefits."

"Free samples, huh?" Stephanie perked up a little at that idea. Stephanie had figured out that now that her credit cards were cut off, her paycheck still wouldn't cover all the things she had to have. Some decent free samples would be nice. She might have to befriend Pam after all. She could be useful, she decided.

Stephanie handed over her money to the cashier, and she and Pam took a table near the back.

"So, since you've worked here awhile, you probably know just about everybody," Stephanie said in a casual voice. "Like Jonathan Baur?"

Pam nodded and took a bite of her sandwich.

"Tell me," Stephanie went on. "What's his story? What department does he work in?"

Pam swallowed, but before she could speak, Jonathan himself walked in.

"Catch you later," Stephanie said, jumping up and walking over to him.

She sidled up next to Jonathan. "Hi, Jonathan. We meet again," Stephanie cooed in her sweetest voice.

"And this is Graves Hall, which houses Wilder University's state-of-the-art computer department," Terry said to Sean Fletcher and

Rob Delucca as they paused on the steps of the imposing building. "I'm not a computer buff, but I do know it's been completely revamped and that they've just installed all kinds of impressive equipment. A vast network, fiber optics, the works."

"This whole campus is pretty impressive," Sean replied. "I appreciate your showing us around."

"No problem," Terry said. "It's the least I can do, considering the time you're giving to all of us."

"Oh, wow. Aren't you Sean Fletcher?" Several female students came running up the stairs behind them.

Sean turned and smiled easily. "That I am. And this is Rob Delucca, art director extraordinaire. And who are you?"

"I'm Theresa; this is Rhonda; this is Wendy," one of the young women said breathlessly, giving Rob a glance, but then turning her full attention on Sean. After getting Sean's autograph, they moved off and Terry could hear one of them saying, "Unbelievable. We actually got Sean Fletcher's autograph. Wait till I show my roommate. She'll be insanely jealous."

"You're causing an unbelievable stir around here," Terry said to his guests. "Do you ever get tired of signing so many autographs?"

Sean shrugged. "Not really. I appreciate my fans. They're why I'm in the business."

They continued around the quad.

"I'd like to show you the Rockhausen Library next, better known as the Rock," Terry said. "Since it's exam time, most of Wilder's student population is holed up in there."

As they started up the steps, Terry looked up to see Nancy Drew coming out the front door. She was wearing a deep burgundy sweater, and her legs looked a mile long in her slim-fitting jeans. Terry felt a blast of pleasure as she walked up and said hello.

"Hi, Nancy," Terry said, taking a deep breath of her lightly scented perfume. "You remember Sean Fletcher and Rob Delucca."

Whoa, she's beautiful. I wonder if she has a boyfriend, Terry thought. In the next second, he shook his head. Of course she does, you idiot. She's only one of the most gorgeous women at Wilder.

"I've been giving Sean and Rob the grand tour around Wilder—you know, science building, the computer center, and now the library," Terry said, his eyes still locked onto Nancy.

If she noticed, she didn't acknowledge it. She simply smiled in an offhanded way that lit up her blue eyes.

"So Terry's been giving you the Wilder tour," she said. "Don't let the official ivy-covered buildings fool you. There's more to

Wilder than gorgeous manicured lawns and the academic grind. In fact, a bunch of us are going rollerblading tonight. If you really want a glimpse of student life, why don't you join us? We'd love to have you," Nancy said.

"Why not?" Sean said.

"I'd love to come, too," Rob said, "but unfortunately, I've got plans. An old friend is coming out from Chicago to meet me for dinner." He glanced at his watch. "As a matter of fact, if you'll excuse me, I've got to run a couple of errands before then."

As Rob took off, Terry noticed that several students had gathered around them on the steps. It had been like this all morning. Wherever Sean went on the Wilder campus, he caused a commotion.

It seems that Nancy's fallen under his spell, too, Terry thought when he saw how she was looking at Sean. So Sean has another groupie. Well, there was no getting around it—Sean was good-looking, and he had that no-fail celebrity magnet thing going. But then Terry heard Nancy say, "Sean, I know this is coming out of the blue, but I've got something important to talk about with you."

Terry listened as she told Sean about an encounter with someone named Mrs. Vandenbrock, the subject of some journalism project of Nancy's. He didn't see what her school project had to do with Sean until Nancy told him about her theory regarding Lauren Fletcher and Mrs. Vandenbrock. Then Terry found himself paying attention.

"I know it's a total long shot," Nancy said. "But look at these. See for yourself."

She rummaged through her backpack and handed Sean several newspaper articles she'd copied. Terry could tell by Sean's expression that his interest was piqued.

"This is very interesting," Sean said, studying the articles.

"Sean Fletcher!" a high-pitched voice broke into their conversation.

Terry was suddenly aware that several more students had closed in around them, and he saw that Sean was becoming uncomfortable.

"I think we could use some privacy," Sean said in a low voice to Nancy. He pointed to the building across the way. "My rental car is over there near the political science building. Do you have time to drive somewhere so we can discuss this further?"

Nancy nodded. "Sure. I've got a little time. Terry, want to join us?"

Terry glanced at his watch and felt a knot of disappointment that had nothing to do with his curiosity about Lauren Fletcher. "No, I can't. I've got a meeting with my projectionist for the film society. But go on. I'm sure you two have a lot to discuss."

As Terry watched them climb into Sean's

rental car, he felt his chest tighten. They were laughing, their heads close together.

Admit it, Terry said to himself. You, my friend, are jealous of Sean. Well, at least I have another chance to be with Nancy tonight at the skating party. Too bad Sean's coming, too.

CHAPTER 7

Jake Collins slumped into a sofa in the Student Union and closed his eyes. The frenetic rock music playing on the loudspeaker provided a fitting background for the tumult playing in his mind. He'd turned in his class paper, but it wasn't his best work, and he knew it.

Jake had put in a lot of time on two recent articles he'd written for the *Wilder Times,* one on racism and another great piece he'd written with Nancy on animal rights. And he'd been pleased with the result.

Ever since then, however, the words just hadn't been flowing. He couldn't even seem to write a simple class paper. Maybe he'd been trying too hard, Jake decided. He was glad Nancy had called and invited him to go skating that night. It was probably just the thing he needed. An evening of relaxation—and of Nancy.

Cheered by the thought, Jake sat up just as Will Blackfeather strode in through the side door of the Student Union. Seeing Jake, Will wandered over, dumped his bookbag on the low coffee table, and took a seat on the sofa across from Jake.

"How go the study wars?" Will asked. "Or should I ask?"

"I think I've had it. I surrender," Jake said.

Will chuckled as he shrugged off his motorcycle jacket. "Here." He pulled a stainless steel thermos and two paper cups out of his backpack. "I had this filled at Java Joe's on my way over. Suck this down and see if you don't find hope for survival."

Jake sat up. "At last. A reason for living," he joked. He wrapped his hands around his cup of coffee and sipped slowly. "Yes, I believe I might live through exams after all."

Will nodded. "Good. I'm glad. Now, how about a game of pool?"

Jake stood up. "Sounds good."

They walked downstairs to the pool room and took the first open pool table where they started a spirited game. As they played, Jake felt himself relax.

"So aside from the dreaded *S* word, what else have you been up to?" he asked Will as soon as he had a comfortable lead.

Will positioned his cue and dropped two balls in the side pocket.

"Not much," he said, grinning triumphantly. "How about you? Been seeing much of Nancy?"

Jake frowned and lined up his shot. "Things are going well enough." He pulled back his stick—and missed. "The only real problem is that we're both so busy, we don't get to see each other as much as we'd like."

"Oh, things will probably ease up after exams," Will said. He watched as his shot went wide.

"Tough luck," Jake said.

"So what about you? How are you and George doing?"

Will pursed his lips and rubbed his jaw as he studied his next move. "Not great," he admitted. "I thought things were pretty near perfect, but then, I don't know. Something changed. She's been acting different, somehow."

"In what way?"

"Different, as in quieter, withdrawn. Not her usual style," Will said. "Usually, she's got so much to say and has so much energy, I have trouble keeping up with her. Something's definitely bothering her."

"Any ideas?" Jake asked.

Will shook his head. "Not a clue. She doesn't seem to want to talk about it."

"Well, we're all pretty much under the gun with exams and studying. Maybe she's keyed up about that," Jake ventured.

"Could be," Will said, sounding unconvinced. "I'm glad that we're all going out rollerblading tonight. Maybe she'll let me in on what's going on with her."

Jake nodded. "Yeah, I'm looking forward to it myself. I'll have a chance to see Nancy—and it'll feel good to blow off some steam."

With that, Jake sank another ball into the side pocket. "Game. I win," he said triumphantly.

"Save a guy's life with a cup of well-timed coffee, and look how he repays you," Will joked, shaking Jake's hand.

After Sean shut off the engine, Nancy sat quietly for a moment. Now that she was sitting alone with Sean in the parking lot by the lake on campus, she couldn't help wondering if maybe she made a mistake telling the actor what she was thinking. After all, she had no proof and very little information to go on.

"I know this must be hard for you," Nancy began. "Let me know if you just want me to back off on all of this, and I will."

Sean looked at her, the shadows playing off his angular face. "No," he said in a low voice. "I've wondered about my mother all of my life. I made up my mind that no matter how painful it got, I'd press on, and I wouldn't let anything stop me. What do you have?"

Nancy handed him the wedding announcement she'd copied from the microfilm. "Not a whole lot here," she confessed. "But enough to keep me wondering."

She looked at Sean's handsome face and hoped that her efforts might somehow help him. For a guy who had so much—fame, connections, and money—he seemed so vulnerable.

While Sean studied the announcement, he sank back in the tan leather. Then he looked at the other articles she'd handed him. "I don't know. It does seem pretty unlikely that Mrs. Vandenbrock and my mother might be the same person. Their worlds are so far apart. What else do you know about Mrs. Vandenbrock?"

"Not much," Nancy said unhappily, thinking about her profile for her class. But she wasn't about to bore Sean with her problem.

"She invited me to her house, but she cut me off while I was trying to interview her. Then I thought maybe my luck had changed this morning when I saw her in her limo in town. I asked her to let me finish the interview, but she absolutely wouldn't hear of it. She rolled up her window and drove away."

"Well, I can understand some of that," Sean said. "It seems like it would be fun always having people recognize you. But you find yourself getting protective of your privacy."

Nancy nodded. "I guess being a celebrity, you'd know." She looked at him a minute and asked, "Does the name Leila Greer mean anything to you?"

Sean shook his head. "Well, that wasn't my mother's maiden name, if that's what you're thinking. But then again, I suppose she could have changed her name after leaving Hollywood."

He held up the newspaper photo again. "And though this isn't a very clear picture, I definitely see a resemblance. I don't know, Nancy. Maybe you have stumbled onto something here."

Nancy furrowed her brow. "Well, I don't want to get too excited. That photo isn't enough to go on. But the woman in it looks like your mom did in the movie last night. Do you have any personal photos of your mom?"

Sean looked pained. "No," he said with a sigh. "The divorce was incredibly bitter. Over the years I'd ask my dad about her, but he'd never talk. He'd completely cut me off. I was so curious. I even started asking the housekeepers about her. They'd been ordered not to talk about her either. But one of our housekeepers told me that Dad burned my mother's pictures right after she disappeared."

"It's good they didn't burn all the film footage," Nancy said sympathetically. "It must have been difficult for you growing up, not knowing anything about your mother except what you saw on old movies."

"It wasn't easy." Sean shook his head. His voice grew bitter. "I used to watch those movies just to see what she looked like. I'd play the videos over and over, and I'd freeze the frames just to study her face. Her film roles are all the memories I have of her."

Nancy was startled when he sat up abruptly. "Well, I don't want to wait and wonder any longer. I've been looking for my mother for years. Let's go see Mrs. Vandenbrock right away. I've got to know if there's any truth to this."

George stood outside Bess's door and knocked. She glanced at her sportswatch. Was Bess sleeping in this late? After waiting a moment, George knocked again.

"Coming," Bess yelled.

As Bess slowly opened the door, George could see her kicking at clothes that were piled on the floor like snowdrifts.

"Oh, hi, George. Come in. Ignore the mess," Bess grumbled. "Seems that almost overnight my roomie, formerly known as Ms. Neatness Personified, has morphed into the biggest slob."

George laughed as she stepped over a pile into the room. "Now, here's a switch: Leslie's side of the room looking like Mount Disaster and yours like an ad for Organization Unlimited."

"I don't know what's happened to me," Bess confessed. "But I just got this weird urge to clean. I've been at it all morning. Something about Leslie's mess makes me want to retaliate by cleaning up my side."

George sat down on Bess's neatly made bed. She nodded toward Bess's stack of books and papers on her desk.

"Hitting the books?" she asked.

"Yeah, that too. I've been logging in so many hours with my bio book, I'm beginning to frighten myself," Bess joked. She sat down at her desk, turning her chair to face George. Her blue eyes grew wide. "Uh-oh, I'm in danger of turning into Leslie."

George grinned at her cousin. "Better not. One Leslie around here is all anybody can take."

Bess tilted her head and absently chewed on a piece of her blond hair. "Love. It does the strangest things to people."

"You can say that again."

Bess glanced up at George. "So, what brings you here?" she asked.

George took a deep breath. "I was just passing by. Well, actually, I wanted to talk to you." She paused. "It's about me and Will."

Bess sat up and looked closely at her cousin. "You guys didn't have a fight or anything, did you?"

"No, nothing like that." George stared up at

the ceiling. How could she explain what she was feeling? "We really never fight. In fact, everything seems perfect. That's the trouble."

Bess nodded. "Are you tired of Will?" she asked.

George shook her head vehemently. "Not in the least. I love to be around him. I get this warm, amazing glow just knowing he's there. Know what I mean?"

Bess nodded. "That's how I feel when I'm with Paul. Okay, so you're not fighting. You're not tired of him. You love being around him. What's the deal?"

"That's what I was trying to tell you. The fact that there isn't a problem *is* the problem."

Bess scratched her head. "Well, then, call me clueless, because I can't figure out what you're talking about."

George grinned and ran her fingers through her short, dark hair. "I know it doesn't make sense. I can't figure it out myself. That's why I'm here. I guess I've been thinking a lot lately. Trouble is, the more I think, the more confused I get. I mean, I love Will, but I know our future together could be complicated."

"News flash: Every relationship is complicated," Bess pointed out.

George went on. "I know that. But you have to admit that when a relationship starts to get serious, things don't seem to be so simple anymore."

"Maybe," Bess acknowledged. "But who says you and Will have to be serious? So what if you've been dating awhile. You're still in college. You should just be having a great time and enjoying getting to know someone. You don't have to start messing around with something that's just fine as it is by thinking about the future. I don't see why you're making a big thing of it."

"I know," George said, scrutinizing the ceiling again. "Maybe I am borrowing trouble."

Bess stood up. "I happen to think you are. The way I see it is that you and Will love each other. It's not like you're signing up for a lifetime commitment tomorrow. You should relax about the future and just have fun."

"Like it's that simple," George said.

Bess nodded and snapped her fingers. "Yes, it is that simple. And now that I've helped you set that straight, I need your help."

With that, she threw open the door of her closet. George's eyes almost popped out. Every article of clothing in Bess's closet was neatly hung. Her jackets were all together, next to her pants and blouses. Her nicer dresses were hung in garment bags. Even Bess's shoes seemed to be standing at attention in orderly rows along the floor.

"I don't believe what I'm seeing," George said with a low whistle. "Your closet is clean.

I ought to take a picture to send to your folks back home."

Bess laughed and nodded. "It still doesn't help me out of my dilemma. Even though I can find everything, I can't figure out what I should wear tonight. Help me decide."

George shook her head. It was impossible for Bess to be serious about anything for too long. But she realized that a good dose of Bess was just what she needed. Her fears about Will weren't completely put to rest, but she had to admit that she did feel better.

"All right," she said, poking her head into Bess's closet. "Although I'm probably the last person who should be your fashion consultant. Let's see what you have here."

CHAPTER 8

"Well, I don't want to be too much of a pessimist, but I've definitely been here, done this before," Nancy said as she gazed up at the imposing gate with its ornate *V* at the top. The vast expanse of green lawn seemed to go on forever until it met up with the massive Vandenbrock mansion. "Let's see how long I go this time before I get kicked out again."

"*One* person lives here?" Sean asked.

Nancy nodded. "Well, Mrs. Vandenbrock and several servants."

"Definitely an impressive place," Sean said, craning his neck to see everything.

"Check out that turret—and those columns. They must be made of marble." Nancy said. "The house is even more amazing inside." She pressed the intercom button. "Mrs. Vandenbrock has some beautiful antiques. Of course,

I didn't get to see all that much since I was whisked out so quickly."

"Let's hope things go differently today," Sean said forcefully.

Nancy was struck at how nervous the actor seemed. She could see tension all across his face. It was obvious that this meant a great deal to him. Oh, please, she thought as they waited for a reply from the house, let Mrs. Vandenbrock at least see us.

At last, a crackly male voice came through the speaker. "Yes?"

"My name is Nancy Drew, and I've come to see Mrs. Vandenbrock," Nancy said. "I've brought a visitor with me, Sean Fletcher."

"I'm very sorry, Ms. Drew," the voice replied. "This is not a good time."

Nancy leaped for the intercom. "Well, when would be a good time?" There was silence from the intercom. "Look, did you hear me? I've brought Sean *Fletcher.*" She said the last word loudly and distinctly.

"Please wait a moment," the voice replied.

Nancy and Sean exchanged looks. "I guess that was her butler," Nancy said.

"I hope she'll see us," Sean said.

Poor Sean. He looked so ill at ease, Nancy thought. Well, she couldn't blame him. In the next few minutes he just might come face-to-face with his long-lost mother. That would be enough to unnerve anyone!

The speaker crackled. "I'm very sorry, but Mrs. Vandenbrock is not receiving visitors today. She asked me to thank you for stopping by."

Nancy watched as the color drained from Sean's face. No, this couldn't happen! They were being turned away.

She sprang to action and pressed the intercom button. "Oh, but you don't understand," she said in an urgent voice. "We absolutely must see Mrs. Vandenbrock. It's very important."

"I'm sorry. I'm afraid that will be impossible." The voice was detached and impersonal.

This time Sean stepped up to the intercom. "I really must see her. You have no idea how critical this is."

"And I must insist that you leave now, or I shall be forced to call the police." The butler's voice took on a chilly, clipped tone.

Sean turned to Nancy, desperation evident in his eyes. "I can't believe this. She's got to see us. This might be my mother, and I have to find out."

Nancy tried to think of something to say. There simply had to be a way to get Mrs. Vandenbrock to talk to Sean.

Sean's eyes flashed. "Well, I don't care if she doesn't want to see me. I want to see her." He stood back and sized up the tall, spiked gate. "All I have to do is find a tree or something and get over this gate and then I'll force my way in."

Nancy shook her head and placed her hand on his arm. "Sean," she said. "I know this is important to you, but that isn't the way. For one thing, Mrs. V. might not even be your mother. And the last thing you need is to be arrested for trespassing."

"I don't care," Sean replied.

"Aside from that," Nancy went on. "If she is your mother, your barging in on her isn't going to make things easier."

Sean heaved a sigh and stood deep in thought, appearing to consider what Nancy said. Finally, he nodded. "You're right. But somehow, I will find a way to see her."

"I know we'll figure out something. Let's go," Nancy said.

As they turned to walk away, Nancy looked back at the huge mansion. Suddenly a movement in the leaded glass window beside the front door caught her eye. No doubt about it, someone was watching them!

"Oh, no," Eileen wailed as she jiggled the plug on her blow-dryer. "My dryer just fritzed out on me. Great. I'll just go to the party as a wethead." She tapped the blow-dryer a couple of times against the bathroom sink and flipped the switch again. It was no use. Her dryer was kaput.

"Don't worry about it," Kara replied. "I'm finished. You can use mine."

"Thanks," Eileen said gratefully, fluffing at her wet hair in the steamed-up mirror. She reached over for Kara's dryer. "I can't believe how everything's going wrong tonight. Maybe this is a sign."

"Everything will be fine," Liz said. She applied generous amounts of mascara to her eyelashes. "We are going to be dressed to kill. And we'll dance and have the time of our lives."

Eileen rolled her eyes. "I shouldn't have let you guys talk me into this mess. I should have listened to myself and gone rollerblading," she grumbled before flipping the switch of the blow-dryer.

Kara punched her playfully on the shoulder as she walked out. In the next minute, she yelled loudly enough to be heard over the whirring of hair dryers, "Anyone seen my high heels?"

After Eileen finished drying and styling her hair, she leaned closer to the mirror and started applying her makeup. When she was finished, she went to her bedroom, slipped on her dress and stepped back to check out her reflection in her mirror. And she was pleased with what she saw. Her dress was a pale, delicate pink with a satiny skirt and a cut velvet bodice. The shimmery garment showed off Eileen's athletic build. Her hair curled under perfectly, her eyes sparkled, and the dress made the whole picture one of perfection.

"Eileen, you look stunning," Kara said as Eileen emerged from her room.

Eileen smiled. "Thanks."

"Emmet will think he's a lucky guy when he gets his first look at you."

"Okay, so maybe you were right that I should go to this dance," Eileen conceded. "It is kind of fun to get dressed up once in a while." And though she didn't want to admit it out loud, she dared to hope that maybe her blind date wouldn't be so bad after all.

It wasn't long before Tim Downing came to pick up Kara. He was wearing a black tuxedo with a richly colored brocade vest that complemented Kara's dress, and Eileen couldn't help thinking what a handsome couple they made as they left. Daniel came for Liz, and they also swept off into the night.

As each minute passed Eileen became more and more tightly wound. What would her date be like? While she waited, she closed her eyes and pictured herself on the arm of some to-die-for guy. Time continued to drag on and still there was no sign of Eileen's date.

"I wonder where he is," Eileen said to herself, glancing at the clock hanging on the wall.

Just then there was a knock on the suite door, Eileen's head snapped up. This was it, she thought as she opened it. But it was Jake Collins, not her date, who walked in. Jake was dressed casually, and he carried a pair of in-line skates over one shoulder.

"Hi, Eileen. Hey, great dress," he said. "Where's Nancy? I'm here to pick her up for the skating party."

Eileen stepped back, trying to conceal her disappointment. "Um, thanks for the compliment. Nancy? I haven't seen her for hours," she said.

Jake frowned. "That's strange," he said. "I was supposed to meet her here. At least, that's what I thought she said. I wonder where she could be."

Eileen glanced at the clock for the umpteenth time. "And I'm wondering where my date could be."

She sighed and nibbled off some of her lipstick.

Jake set his skates down on the beat-up coffee table. "We'll just wait together, I guess."

"It might be a long wait. Maybe you and I have both been stood up," she joked.

Before Jake could reply, someone knocked at the door. With her heart in her throat, Eileen ran over to open it. This time, it was a good-looking guy whom Eileen had never seen before. He, too, was carrying a pair of in-line skates that dangled almost to the ground by long, tangled laces.

"Hi. My name's Terry Schneider," the guy said. "I'm here to pick up Nancy Drew for the rollerblading party."

Eileen's glance darted from Terry's face to Jake's. A muscle twitched in Jake's jaw, and Eileen could plainly see that he was none too pleased at the strange guy's announcement.

"Funny you should say that," Jake said evenly, coolly checking out Terry. "I'm here to pick up Nancy as well. But the weird thing is, she's not here. So I'm not sure where that leaves either of us."

Was Nancy playing some sort of game with these guys? Eileen thought frantically. But no, that didn't seem like Nancy at all.

Eileen tried desperately to think of something to say, but before she could come up with anything, there was another knock on the door. Terry opened it.

"I'm here for Eileen O'Connor," a familiar voice said.

Eileen nearly fainted when she saw who came in the door wearing a tuxedo and brandishing a corsage. It was the same huge guy from the gym who'd knocked her down!

Jake opened the door of the Student Union for Nancy and Terry, and he followed them over to where George, Will, and Andy sat clumped together in a small seating area.

As Jake walked along, he couldn't help staring at Terry, wondering about him and about why Nancy had shown up so late. Sure, she'd mentioned having some adventure with Sean Fletcher at the Vandenbrock mansion, but that was about all he'd learned. Well, that and how it came about that Terry had turned up to join the rollerblading party.

While Nancy had been gathering her skates, Terry had explained to Jake that Nancy had invited both Terry and Sean along, but that Sean had been too tired and depressed about his mother to join them.

"Sorry I'm so late," Nancy was now saying to everyone. "But you wouldn't believe the afternoon I've had!"

"No problem," George said, standing up and picking up her skates by their laces. "Will and I were late getting here ourselves. We had to scrounge all over the place to find someone to lend Will skates."

"Reva's not coming," Andy said. "She's been fighting a cold, and I think the cold's winning."

"Too bad," Nancy said sympathetically. "She's going to miss the fun. Well, onward."

The group headed outside and sat down to put on their skates and protective gear.

Will stood up unsteadily. "I haven't rollerbladed in ages."

George zoomed up next to him and grabbed

his hand. "Well, get ready because you've got some catch-up work to do."

With that, she raced down the Walk daring everyone to keep up with her. Will and Andy shot after her, and soon they were laughing and trying to outdo each other with fancy turns and stunts.

Jake skated up next to Nancy. "So what happened this afternoon?" he asked.

Nancy shook her head so that her hair rippled in the moonlight. "Oh, Jake, it's all so complicated. Mind if I tell you later?"

Jake shrugged and tried to tell himself that it didn't matter. A few minutes later he also tried to convince himself that it didn't matter that Nancy and Terry were now skating side by side. As Jake skated along, he could hear Nancy talking about the day's adventures. It was clear to Jake that Terry already knew something about it all.

Terrific, he thought moodily. I'm competing against a movie star named Sean and a guy named Terry who rollerblades like a pro. Is this fun or what?

By staying right behind the two of them, Jake heard Nancy explain to Terry how they'd decided to go to the mansion after Nancy had shown Sean some photos. She described the conversation with the butler over the intercom and Mrs. Vandenbrock's refusal to see them.

"And so Sean wanted to climb the fence,

but I persuaded him that it probably wasn't the brightest idea and . . ." Nancy said. The rest of her sentence was lost to Jake as she and Terry turned the corner by the clock tower.

Jake fell back and skated slowly. He was fast losing enthusiasm for the whole in-line skating idea.

Great, Collins, he mumbled to himself. Some killer evening this is turning out to be. Maybe you just should have stationed yourself in your cubicle and written something to impress your editor instead.

Just then Nancy appeared from around the corner and made her way toward him.

"Hi, Jake," she called. "Sorry. Didn't mean to leave you back here. We got going so fast. Terry is really good on skates."

Jake smiled a tight smile as she did a little spin in front of him. "Well, you're here now," he said.

Nancy skated up next to him. "You having fun?" she asked, slipping her cold hand into his.

Jake nodded and tried to warm her hand. "You bet," he said quickly.

Amazing, he thought, the effect this woman had on him. He started wobbling on his skates, and his blood began to course faster through his veins. He wanted to take her into his arms and kiss away any images she might have of Terry or Sean.

Nancy snuggled up closer, and then she put her arm around his waist. "Come on," she said, her blue eyes dancing. "Let's have some fun."

As Jake felt himself being swept along, his mood lifted. He held Nancy close and breathed in the scent of her lemony shampooed hair and smiled.

Now this is more like it, he thought happily. Check it out, Terry, he wanted to shout.

CHAPTER 9

Bess looked happily around her at Les Peches. The Kappa-Alpha party had just gotten under way, and the banquet room in the elegant restaurant was filled with laughing, chattering students dressed up and looking their best. She sat at a pink linen–covered table near the door and glanced over at Paul. He was amazing in his tuxedo with his golden hair glowing in the candlelight.

But where was Eileen? Bess couldn't wait to see Eileen's face when she came in on the arm of one of the handsomest guys on campus. Emmet will change her mind about giving up on dating, Bess thought with satisfaction.

She kept her eye on the door, and at last she saw Eileen walk into the room. But what was this? Instead of looking radiant, Eileen was looking depressed. Bess watched in puzzlement as Emmet tried to hold the door open

107

for her, but Eileen held the door herself, brushed past him, and tilted her chin up haughtily.

"Believe me, I'm definitely in shape enough to get it myself," Bess heard Eileen's crisp voice drift across the room.

"Now what's going on with them?" Bess asked aloud.

"Uh-oh," said Kara, who was sitting across from Bess. "This is not a good sign."

"You said it," Bess muttered. "Looks like disaster on the dating front."

"You've got that right. Emmet doesn't look very happy," Paul said.

"*Emmet* doesn't look happy?" Bess exclaimed. "Check out Eileen! She looks like she would sooner deck Emmet than dance with him."

Eileen walked toward Bess's table and thumped her evening bag on her chair.

"Hello, everybody," she said stiffly.

"Hi," Bess said. "Hi, Emmet."

"Shall we get these parched women something to drink?" Paul asked Emmet.

"What? Oh, sure," Emmet muttered distractedly, and the two walked toward the drinks table.

As soon as the guys were out of earshot, Bess leaned over to Eileen. "What in the world is wrong?" she asked.

Kara added, "Here we line up a to-die-for guy, and you look miserable."

Eileen smoothed her dress and adjusted the neckline. Her eyes didn't quite meet her friends', and Bess could see that she was pale, her freckles standing out more than usual.

"I think this is some kind of sicko cosmic joke," Eileen said flatly. "Your to-die-for Emmet happens to be the very same ape who nearly killed me in the gym this afternoon."

Bess frowned. "What are you talking about?"

"He practically mowed me down. Well, it was sort of an accident," Eileen admitted. "We kind of collided with each other. I got angry because I'd already had a run-in with another jerk who stole my Nautilus machine, and I said something. A gentleman would have just ignored it. But Emmet came back with some rude comments. Anyway, he was about the last guy I wanted to see tonight. But here we are."

"Oh, Eileen, Emmet is a nice guy. He's probably forgotten about the whole thing by now," Bess said.

Eileen shook her head. "*I* haven't forgotten, and he hasn't said a word since he picked me up."

"Paul mentioned that he's pretty keyed up about some paper he had to write," Bess said. "That's probably why he's so quiet."

Eileen scowled. "I don't think it has to do

with any paper. If you want to know the truth, I think Emmet's as bummed at being stuck with me as I am with him."

Bess shook her head. "I don't believe any of this."

"Well, it's not your fault. I know you guys tried," Eileen said. "I told you: This dating thing just doesn't work for me."

"Give Emmet a chance. He's a really nice guy," Bess said.

A short while later Emmet and Paul returned with tall, fruity drinks in frosted glasses. Emmet set one down in front of Eileen, who didn't even acknowledge it. She turned away and pretended to admire the decorations. Bess noticed that Emmet sat down as far from Eileen as he could. She gave Paul a small kick under the table and mouthed, "Help!"

Paul looked grim, and he began to work hard to draw Eileen and Emmet into conversation. Bess could see that he was struggling to find a topic that would interest both of them. At first he was rewarded with stony silence. Kara and Tim began to pick up the threads, and slowly Eileen and Emmet began to respond.

"Bess has been working on a one-act play over at Hewlitt," Paul said, taking up another topic.

"It's kind of artsy," Bess said.

"Artsy, huh," Emmet said neutrally.

"What's wrong with artsy?" Eileen challenged. "Beats spending your life hanging around with jocks who never do anything but work out and grunt and sweat."

Oh, Eileen, this isn't a war, Bess moaned inwardly as she caught Emmet's thin smile.

"Oh, you'd be surprised at the things jocks do besides hang out at gyms," Emmet said. "Have you been to that new impressionist exhibit over at the Longet Gallery? I thought it was great."

Score one point for Emmet, Bess thought, and she glanced at Eileen to see her reaction. She was pleased to note that Eileen actually smiled—a first for the evening. Good, thought Bess. Maybe we'll see a cease-fire in the War Between the Dates!

By the time dinner was served, Bess could tell that Eileen was taking her advice and giving Emmet the benefit of the doubt. And Emmet, for his part, had finally turned to face Eileen, instead of sitting with his back toward her. Bess took a forkful of food and eyed her friends warily. So, they'd established some sort of uneasy truce. Now if only they could keep from killing each other before the evening was through.

"Oh, Ray, I'm so excited for you and the Beat Poets, I won't be able to eat a bite,"

Ginny said, hugging Ray as they walked through the door to Ray's dorm room.

Ray set down the bag containing cartons of Chinese take-out food. "I'm excited, too, but not so excited that I'm going to let perfectly good cashew chicken and fried rice go to waste," he said.

Ginny smiled. "You're right," she said, and tossed her coat over the back of one of Ray's chairs. She scrounged in the bags for some chopsticks, and she and Ray proceeded to open up the cartons of food as they sat down on Ray's bed.

"I still can't believe it," Ginny said, picking up some rice with her chopsticks. "A recording contract!"

"I can't either," Ray said. He took a bite of the cashew chicken and chewed thoughtfully. "It still seems so unreal."

"You've realized a dream!" Ginny exclaimed. She leaned over and kissed Ray.

"We've realized a dream," Ray said firmly, pulling Ginny closer to him. "We're going to have such a good time together, Ginny. I can see it now."

Ginny punched his arm playfully. "You'll be so fabulously successful that you'll be rich before you know it, and the girls will drape themselves all over you. You won't have time for me," she joked.

"I'll always have time for you," Ray insisted.

"And you'll be busy pursuing your own dreams, and I'll be right there for you, just the way you have been for me."

Ginny collected their plates, then reached over to hug Ray again. "Well, right now, all I'm dreaming about is doing well on next week's exams. I'd better start studying, or that will be one dream that I can kiss off."

"Speaking of kissing, that's one thing I want to do right now. We'll buckle down to studying—tomorrow," Ray promised. "Right now I just want to celebrate with you."

"Sounds good to me," Ginny agreed, melting into Ray's arms.

Eileen sat back as the waiter approached to bring them coffee and dessert—a rich, velvety-looking chocolate mousse. Normally, Eileen would have polished off anything remotely resembling chocolate in no time flat, but tonight every bite seemed to stick in her throat.

"Mmmm," Bess said too brightly, taking a huge spoonful. "I think I've died and gone to heaven."

"I've never met anything chocolate I didn't like," agreed Kara.

Eileen managed a weak smile. "It is delicious," she said, trying to be sociable. "Don't you think so, Emmet?" She looked over at Emmet, who'd just picked up his spoon and taken a taste of his dessert.

Emmet nodded but didn't elaborate. He shifted in his seat and pulled at his collar as though he found it uncomfortably tight. Everything about him seemed so forced, Eileen thought, watching him out of the corner of her eye. In fact, the whole evening with him had been awkward. And now it was going from bad to worse.

After the dishes were cleared, more upbeat music began, and couples started to drift out onto the parquet dance floor. Eileen looked at Emmet expectantly, but Emmet merely sipped his coffee moodily and made no move to ask her to dance. Though it was painful, Eileen continued to work to make polite conversation. Emmet answered in monosyllables and stared off into the room.

Finally Eileen decided to take matters into her own hands. "Would you like to dance?"

Emmet started to get up, and when he did, he knocked over his coffee, sending a flood of lukewarm brown liquid cascading over Eileen's dress. Eileen watched in horror as her dress was soaked.

"I'm so sorry," Emmet said, standing up quickly and reaching over with a napkin to try to clean up the mess.

Eileen pulled away angrily. "Haven't you done enough?" she spat out.

This is the last straw, she thought, glaring at

him. Oh, why didn't I listen to myself and stay home instead?

Nancy wriggled her toes in her thick socks and settled comfortably into one of the suite's sofas. She'd had a lot of fun skating with her friends, but now she was tired. It felt good to kick back and wait for her suitemates to return from the formal and tell her all about it.

Noises in the hallway announced that the group was back, and Kara and Casey burst through the lounge door.

"Hi, guys," Nancy said. "How did it go?"

Kara collapsed onto the sofa next to Nancy and kicked off her high heels. "I danced my feet off," she announced.

"It was great," Casey said. She flopped onto the floor and arranged her crushed formal around her as she settled into a cross-legged position. "It was so sweet of Brian to take me. He's a great dancer."

"How did Eileen's big date go?" Nancy asked.

Casey rolled her eyes. "Can you spell disaster?"

"We're talking date from hell," added Kara.

"No way!" Nancy exclaimed. "It sounded like Emmet was perfect for Eileen. What happened?"

"You mean, 'What didn't happen?' " Casey said. "They were growling and snarling at each other all night, and none of us could understand why. I mean, everyone says Emmet's a total sweetheart. He's very good-looking, and Eileen was stunning tonight. He and Eileen seemed like they'd have a lot in common."

"Eileen and Emmet kept facing off at the dinner table, and the evening ended up with Emmet spilling his coffee all over her dress," said Kara. "Luckily the coffee was only lukewarm or she'd also probably be looking for a lawyer right now to sue him for medical damages," Kara added as she rubbed her feet and took down her hair.

"Eileen looked as if she wanted to run him through a wood chipper," Casey added.

Nancy burst into laughter. "I really shouldn't be laughing," she sputtered. "but it does sound like a comedy. Oh, poor Eileen. This will put her off dating forever."

Kara nodded. "Tim and I were taking bets that they'd end up killing each other before the night was over." She stood up. "Well, that's it. I'm turning in. See you guys tomorrow." Yawning audibly, she went to her room.

"So that was our night," Casey said with a shrug. "Now tell me about Sean Fletcher and your afternoon with him."

Nancy drew her knees up and wrapped her arms around them. "Well, it definitely was intriguing. I told Sean my theory that Lauren Fletcher and Mrs. Vandenbrock might be the same person, and he insisted we go to the Vandenbrock mansion. But she wouldn't see us." Nancy went on to explain Sean's reaction to being turned away.

"When I left him, he was pretty upset about the whole thing."

Casey leaned forward. "Wow. Do you really think that Mrs. V. could be Sean's mom?"

Nancy furrowed her brow. "Could be," she said. "I mean, the whole scandal is pretty weird. It doesn't seem impossible that there could be this one more bizarre element to it."

"Wouldn't that be something?" Casey was intrigued. "Do you think Lauren Fletcher killed David Jacobs?"

"I have no idea," Nancy admitted. "I've been turning it over and over in my mind. And I was wondering, though, if Lauren didn't kill him, and he didn't commit suicide, then who did kill him?"

Casey looked thoughtful. Finally she threw up her hands. "I have absolutely no idea. The only person who really had anything to do with the movie that I know of was Erika Swann, and she's never talked about the scandal."

"True," Nancy said.

"Erika's taking me to lunch tomorrow before the final screening of the Sebastian Fletcher film festival," Casey said.

"That's your perfect opportunity!" Nancy exclaimed.

Casey looked puzzled. "Perfect opportunity for what?"

"To ask her about David Jacobs, of course," Nancy said.

"I guess I could bring it up, if she seems open," Casey said. "But what if she won't talk?"

Nancy shook her head. "Well then, I guess we'll never know what happened. David Jacobs's death and Mrs. Vandenbrock's identity just might always remain total mysteries."

CHAPTER 10

"Oh, great. Where did I leave my script?" Bess muttered on Sunday morning as she rummaged through a stack of books on her desk. She caught a glimpse of the time and sighed. "Late for rehearsal again. Brian's absolutely going to kill me."

She scanned her bookshelf hurriedly, then started rummaging through her bookbag. No script. Well, maybe she'd get lucky and Brian would oversleep—just this once. After all, he probably was just as tired as she was from the Kappa-Delt formal the night before.

Finally Bess found her script in the covers bunched at the foot of her bed. After making up her bed, she started toward the door. Just then her eyes strayed over to Leslie's unmade, unslept-in-bed. Not even to come home for the night, Bess thought. This was so unlike her uptight roommate.

Bess paused, then stepped over a mound of Leslie's clothes. She wasn't sure why, but suddenly she felt as though maybe she should wait for Leslie. Maybe something's happened to her, she thought. The next minute she laughed at herself. "Who are you kidding? You know where she is. Leslie spent the night at Nathan's."

Bess glanced over at Leslie's bed again. This was ridiculous. She wasn't Leslie's mother. And furthermore, she was later than ever for rehearsal. She should be walking out that door right now instead of sitting there sticking her nose in her roommate's business.

"Okay, so what if she didn't come home last night? Is it any of your concern?" Bess asked aloud.

Still, Bess's mind plowed on. Nathan was Leslie's first serious boyfriend. And for her to be sleeping with him so soon in their relationship did seem to be rushing things.

"Whatever," Bess mumbled, feeling foolish. She'd better make tracks to the theater. Scrounging under a pile of papers for a pen, Bess scribbled a note on a piece of sticky paper, which she stuck onto the monitor of Leslie's computer.

"Call me as soon as you get this. I'm at Hewlitt. Bess," she wrote.

A few minutes later Bess breezed into the small room where Brian was already reading his part out loud. Brian pounded his fist on the small table that was downstage.

"Consider this, wretched woman, that your cause is already lost," he read dramatically from his book before glancing up at Bess.

Bess smiled apologetically. "I hope you don't mean that," she joked.

"Another day, another credit card payment," Stephanie grumbled as she headed toward the bank of elevators at Berrigan's. Oh, it was going to be a long day. If only she didn't have to work. It was a gorgeous Sunday, and she wanted to be outside relaxing, not facing Mrs. Moreno's sour face.

"Oh, Stephanie, may I see you for a moment?" It was the disapproving voice of Mrs. Caldwell, the personnel director.

"Certainly," Stephanie said, pasting a smile on her face. Spare me from one of your lectures, she mumbled to herself, following Mrs. Caldwell to her office.

Mrs. Caldwell closed the door behind her and turned to face Stephanie.

"I'm afraid things aren't working out quite the way we thought," she began. "Mrs. Moreno—"

"So I'm fired," Stephanie said. She was surprised to find how afraid she was to lose her job. She desperately wanted the money.

Mrs. Caldwell's eyes grew softer behind her

glasses. "No. Berrigan's believes in its employees. After all, we've invested time and money into your training. We believe in making adjustments if that's what's necessary. So, we're transferring you to another department."

"Okay," Stephanie said. Anything had to be better than old ladies' dresses and cranky old Mrs. Moreno.

"But you'll have to work on your attitude, Stephanie. You've been assigned to the toy department," continued Mrs. Caldwell smoothly.

Fine, Stephanie thought. Who cared what department she was in. Work was work. All of it was boring and stupid.

Wishing she had a cigarette, Stephanie walked through cosmetics on her way to the toy department. She ignored Pam as she passed her.

What could be simpler than selling toys? she thought. And, anyway, maybe she'd get lucky and see Jonathan around. The toy department was more centrally located than ladies' dresses.

At least Mr. Barnwell, the manager in toys, didn't appear to have an attitude the size of the State of Texas, Stephanie thought after she introduced herself to him.

"Nicetomeetyou," he said all in one word. "Why don't you walk around here and get oriented to our stock."

Stephanie shrugged and made her way down an aisle, glancing at the toys. Mr. Barnwell must be at least a hundred years old, she thought. As she rounded the corner, she knocked over a display of robot packages.

"Oh, dear," Mr. Barnwell wheezed. "That display took me hours to set up."

"No problem," Stephanie said. She began to pick up the packages. This took hours? she thought. Well, I guess when you're as ancient as he is, anything would take hours.

Mr. Barnwell watched her, and when she was finished, he motioned her over.

Stephanie deliberately took her time going over to him.

Mr. Barnwell narrowed his watery blue eyes. "You'll have to move faster than that, Miss Keats," he said. "This department really gets hopping on Sundays."

"I'm sure I can manage," Stephanie said icily, drawing herself up to her full height.

She stared at Mr. Barnwell with her hands on her hips, daring him to say anything else. He merely sniffed and turned to a stack of receipts on the counter. Finally he drifted away to help some customers.

Stephanie watched as he rang up a sale and she yawned. Oh, when would she be allowed to take a coffee break? Idly, she arranged some stuffed animals on one of the shelves.

Stephanie looked over as a short, pudgy kid walked past her and then headed for the sports equipment. He stopped and picked up a soccer ball. Stephanie caught the dirty look that Mr. Barnwell directed her way.

Sighing loudly, Stephanie walked over to the kid, who'd just picked up a football and was looking at the soccer ball as if trying to decide between them.

"Which is it?" she snapped at the boy, who acted scared and moved away without choosing anything. He and his mother left the toy department.

"Stephanie, the idea is to facilitate a sale, not discourage it," Mr. Barnwell said, watching the potential customers leave. "Really, you'll have to do better than this. Now, look. There's a little boy over there who appears to need help. Quickly now."

Stephanie moved slowly toward the customer. So what if Mr. Barnwell busted something because she didn't move fast enough.

Stephanie looked down at a grubby, small boy who was standing in front of her. He must have been eating a chocolate ice-cream cone earlier because he was still wearing half of it. Ugh, she thought with revulsion. Why doesn't he wipe his filthy little face? Stephanie glanced over at a woman browsing along the computer games shelf who she guessed to be the boy's mother. The woman's back was to them.

"Can I help you?" Stephanie said to the boy. There, was that sweet enough for old man Barnwell?

"Where are the action figures?" the boy asked.

"Action figures, let's see," Stephanie said, scanning the aisles around her. "I don't know. Why don't you go look? I'm sure you'll find them somewhere."

The boy wiped his mouth with the back of his hand. "You're supposed to tell me," he said, not blinking. "You work here, and you get paid to show me."

"Listen, you little—" Stephanie began. But at a glance from Mr. Barnwell, she stopped. "Fine. Let's go."

She started down the first aisle with the boy trailing behind her. Suddenly she heard a loud noise and turning, Stephanie saw that the boy had knocked over a huge display of construction sets. The boxes cascaded onto the floor, several spilling open. Parts flew everywhere.

"There are the action figures," the boy said, his eyes lighting up as he saw the shelf he was looking for.

"Wait right here," Stephanie commanded, and she looked around for his mother. Surely she would tell the boy to pick up the huge mess he'd just made. But instead, she merely glanced over at the spilled toys and continued browsing. Stephanie couldn't believe it. Well, if his mother wasn't going to handle it, Stephanie would.

"Come on. Pick these things up," she snapped at the boy.

"No way," the boy replied. "I don't work here. You do."

"What?" Stephanie couldn't believe her ears. "Pick this stuff up now."

"You're not my mother," the boy said loudly.

His mother came charging up and glared at Stephanie. Then she looked at her son. "Ryan, what is going on here?"

"She's trying to make me do her work and clean this up!" the boy howled.

"You should be ashamed of yourself," the mother said, turning to Stephanie.

"What?" Stephanie shrieked. "He knocked over our display. He should pick it up. What kind of spoiled brat are you raising, anyway?"

Two bright spots appeared on the woman's cheeks. "How dare you?" she sputtered.

"I'm terribly sorry." Mr. Barnwell was over in an instant, soothing the mother and her son. "We'll straighten this mess up. Now, what is it I can help you with?" He led the woman away after he glared meaningfully at Stephanie.

Stephanie spent the next few minutes in the employee rest room, trying to contain her anger. When she returned to the floor, Mr. Barnwell called her over.

"That was inexcusable," he said.

"Oh, puh-leeze," Stephanie countered.

"You're going to stick up for that psycho-brat?"

Mr. Barnwell's eyebrows raised. "He is one of our best customers."

"He deserves a spanking, not a gift certificate," Stephanie said with a sniff.

"That's it," Mr. Barnwell said. "I'm going to Personnel. I won't have you in my department."

Whatever, Stephanie said, watching his retreating back. Who cared about an angry supervisor? She had a more important thing on her mind. The entire morning had passed, and she hadn't seen Jonathan around. Now, where could he be, she wondered.

Paul glanced at his clock, then at his roommate. It was past ten o'clock, and in the whole time Paul had known Emmet, he'd never slept past eight-thirty.

"I'm onto you. You're awake," Paul said to the motionless lump. In answer, he got a groan and some slight movement. "Give it up. I know you're not asleep."

"I am asleep," said the muffled voice. "Leave me alone."

Paul wasn't about to leave it at that. He picked up Emmet's football and pushed Emmet's bed with his foot until Emmet emerged from under his covers.

"What do you want, dirtball?" he growled.

"An explanation about last night," Paul said, tossing him the football.

Emmet slapped the football down with one hand, then sat up. "About what?"

"Well, you're set up with a pretty girl, you're at a fun party, and the two of you look like you should be voted couple of the year. But you can't eat dinner with her without a war erupting," Paul said. "What gives?"

Emmet tossed the football in the air and caught it again. A football, he could handle. Eileen, he couldn't. "Don't ask."

"I just did."

Emmet spun the football on his finger for a moment before answering. "I don't exactly get it myself. I saw her at the gym yesterday morning, and she ran into me. Or maybe I was worrying about my paper and not really paying attention, and I accidentally ran into her. I'm not sure."

"Bess said something about that to me," Paul said. "But so what? An accident."

Emmet shrugged. "That's how I saw it. I was over there in a heartbeat, falling all over myself apologizing and trying to help her up, but she got pretty hostile and said some stuff. I was tired and said some things I shouldn't have, I guess. We really got into it. So when it turned out that Eileen was my blind date, I thought, well, all right. She's pretty cute, and here's a chance to make things okay."

"But it didn't turn out that way," Paul said.

Emmet shook his head. "You saw for yourself. I guess I'd made such a bad first impression, there was no hope for fixing it. It happens to me a lot. I like someone, and I choke. I put my foot in my mouth and blammo, that's it."

He shrugged.

"So you give up like that?" Paul asked.

Emmet lobbed the football at him. "What else am I supposed to do? I've basically ruined any chance I had with Eileen."

"Don't give up so easily," Paul said, tossing the football back. "Some women need some convincing. Take Bess, for instance. She wasn't exactly falling all over me at first. I had to do some persuading."

Emmet grinned. "Well, you do make it sound hopeful. Maybe all's not lost after all."

Nancy ran her brush through her hair so that it fell softly around her shoulders. She glanced at herself in the mirror and frowned at her troubled expression. She wasn't sure why, but she had the oddest feeling that something had been wrong with Jake the night before. Nothing really huge, just—off.

Well, she told her reflection, maybe she had gotten a little caught up in the intrigue swirling around Mrs. Vandenbrock. All those unanswered questions. There was no getting around it: she hadn't been paying much attention to

Jake lately. And now she wanted to do something about it. She'd pay him a surprise visit.

Just as she reached for her sweater, the phone rang and Nancy answered it.

"Hello," Nancy said.

The voice coming over the line was clipped. "Leila Vandenbrock here. Is Nancy Drew there please?"

Nancy clasped the phone tighter. "Uh-hello, Mrs. Vandenbrock," she said, trying to mask her surprise. "This is Nancy. How are you?"

"I'm just fine, thank you, but I do have a few questions for you."

A few questions for me? Nancy wanted to shout. What about the ones I had for you? "I'll try to help you if I can," she replied evenly.

"Tell me about Sean Fletcher," Mrs. Vandenbrock said. "The man you brought to visit me the other day. Is he Sebastian Fletcher's son?"

"Yes, he is," Nancy answered, her heart beating so loudly, she began to wonder if Mrs. V. could hear it.

"Tell me this," Mrs. Vandenbrock continued. "What does he want?"

"Just to meet you," Nancy answered. "I don't know all that much—I've only just met Sean—but I do know he wants to talk to you about something that's been on his mind for a number of years. He's trying to clear up some questions he's had about his mother."

There was a long pause during which Nancy held her breath. Was Mrs. Vandenbrock going to hang up and simply leave her with more unanswered questions?

Finally Mrs. Vandenbrock spoke. "I'd like you to bring Sean to my home," she said simply.

CHAPTER 11

"Okay, so there I am. Dressed up and ready to give this blind date a shot. Can you imagine what it felt like to open the door and find the last guy on earth you ever wanted to see again standing there?" Eileen asked a few of her suitemates, who were gathered around the lounge on Sunday afternoon.

Dawn Steiger, the resident advisor for the floor, took a handful of popcorn Reva had made and eyed Eileen thoughtfully. "So what did you do?" she asked.

Reva laughed. "I'd have turned him away and gone to the party by myself!"

"I'll bet you would have. And that's what I should have done," Eileen said darkly. "I tried to forget about everything, to have a good time, but everything went totally wrong. Emmet acted standoffish all evening. Then he finished things off by completely ruining my dress. I couldn't help wondering if it was deliberate."

Reva shook her head. "That's a drag. But it doesn't make sense. People who know Emmet say he's a really nice guy. Why would he do a number like this on you?"

Eileen shrugged. "I don't know. Maybe he didn't really mean to spill his coffee on me. But it just seems disaster strikes wherever he goes."

"Kind of like the proverbial bull in a china shop?" Casey asked.

"That might be an overstatement, but you get the idea." Eileen was surprised to hear herself laugh. That might have described Emmet. He *was* big, and it did seem as if whenever he turned around, he was knocking something—or someone—over. But then she realized guiltily that she wasn't really telling the whole story.

"Well, he did apologize when he spilled his coffee. Just like he did when he body-slammed me in the gym—and maybe it was me who walked into him, I'm not sure—but everything was still pretty upsetting."

"Well, I really don't get it," Reva cut in. "The guy is terminally good-looking. He seems nice enough. He apologizes when things happen. How about cutting the guy some slack and chalking it up to a couple of accidents that could happen to anyone?"

Eileen frowned. "It's more than the accidents."

"Well, then, what is it?" Dawn asked.

Eileen glanced around at her suitemates. Why were they giving her the third degree? What was this, the Grand Inquisition?

"Emmet's infuriating," Eileen replied, wanting to close off the subject. "It's that simple."

Reva shrugged, and she looked unconvinced.

"I hate to say it," Dawn said. "But I think you like him more than you want to let on."

"What? Are you nuts?" Eileen said heatedly. She shook her head. "I can't stand him. I don't ever want to hear the name Emmet Lehman again as long as I live. I mean it. I really do."

"To more or less quote William Shakespeare, 'Methinks the lady doth protest too much,'" Casey said with a smile.

"I agree with old William. And I think you should see Emmet again," Reva said. "Give him a chance to show his stuff without the other incidents getting in the way."

"No." Eileen was adamant. "I'm not going to ask for more trouble. I've had enough, thank you. I should have stuck to my guns and stayed home, or at least gone out rollerblading."

"He didn't kiss you good night, did he?" Reva asked. "Maybe that's what you're really mad about."

Eileen couldn't believe what she was hearing. This whole conversation had gone from ridiculous to outrageous! She opened her mouth to shoot down Reva, but she couldn't put her frustration into words. Glaring helplessly, Eileen stormed out of the lounge and slammed the door to her room.

Nancy looked at her watch, and stood up from her seat in the front parlor of the Vandenbrock mansion. She walked around the vast room. Her footsteps echoed on the parquet floor as she studied the beautiful paintings hanging on the walls and admired the cool marble statues placed around the room. From time to time, she glanced uneasily at the carved oak doors to the library where Sean and Mrs. Vandenbrock had been talking for nearly an hour now.

"I'd give anything to be a fly on the wall," Nancy mumbled. "What is going on in there?" Each minute that passed made Nancy want to burst into the library and find out what happened.

Nancy wandered over to the leaded-glass window and looked out onto the formal garden. It was so beautiful. If she weren't so curious about what was going on in the library, she was sure she would have really enjoyed this rare opportunity to relax.

"Miss Drew, Mrs. Vandenbrock has asked

me to show you into the library now," the butler said.

Nancy followed him eagerly, as he drew open the heavy door. Inside the library, she could see that Mrs. Vandenbrock and Sean were sitting on a small damask sofa in front of a fireplace with a burning fire. They were talking, and Nancy saw that Sean was holding one of Mrs. Vandenbrock's heavily jeweled hands. As Nancy walked in, Sean met her gaze. His look of deep sadness didn't escape Nancy.

"Nancy, please come join us," Mrs. Vandenbrock said.

Nancy was on pins and needles. Well, was she Sean's mother, or wasn't she? It was all Nancy could do to contain herself and not to burst out with the question.

Sean stood. "Nancy, this is my aunt Leila," he said, his voice heavy with meaning. His eyes met Nancy's, and she felt her breath catch in her throat.

"Your aunt?" she asked. She'd been so sure after Mrs. Vandenbrock's call that she was Sean's mother.

"Leila Vandenbrock is Lauren Fletcher's younger sister," Sean explained. "I never knew my mother had a sister."

"Greer was the last name of my first husband, whom I divorced before meeting Wendell Vandenbrock," Mrs. Vandenbrock said. She glanced at Sean. "As I told Sean, after the scandal in Hollywood, Lauren came to Chicago to live with me and my first husband.''

Nancy's eyes darted from Sean to Mrs. Vandenbrock. There was still one thing missing, and she had to know.

"So where is Lauren now?" she blurted out.

Sean suddenly stood up. "If you ladies will excuse me, I think I need some air."

With that, Sean walked quickly out of the library. Nancy blinked and turned back to Mrs. Vandenbrock.

Leila Vandenbrock sighed deeply. "I'm afraid that my sister is dead."

Bess opened the door to her room. Leslie was there, sitting in her usual place at her desk, her head bent forward as she worked. The scene looked familiar.

"Hello, Leslie," Bess said, trying to sound casual.

"Hi, Bess," Leslie kept studying.

"It's nice to see you," Bess said. She dropped her books loudly on her desk.

Leslie read a few more lines before setting down her papers and turning around to face Bess. "Is something bothering you?"

"What?" Bess asked, blinking. Was she that easy to read?

Leslie tugged at her ponytail and cleared her throat. "Okay, I think I know what you're thinking, and you're wrong. It may look like it, but I didn't sleep with Nathan. I might not have been going at things in my usual way, but I haven't been as wild as it might seem."

Bess nodded. "Well, I know it's none of my business, but I did wonder when you didn't come home last night."

Leslie grinned. "Yeah, I can imagine. But it wasn't like that at all. Nathan and I ended up at the Cave, and we got to talking. I guess we got caught up and talked all night. I couldn't believe it when we stepped outside and realized it was dawn."

Bess laughed. "Time flies, and all that, huh?"

"Yeah," Leslie said. "It's been a lot of fun letting go and cutting loose. I've been a drudge for far too long, I know it."

"Well, there's nothing wrong with having fun, but I guess it's all a balancing act," Bess said.

Leslie's eyebrows raised. "As if I ever thought I'd hear you, Bess Marvin, say that!"

"I never thought I would hear myself say that," Bess admitted. She looked at her perfectly made bed and her neat side of the room. "To tell you the truth, I've been surprising myself quite a bit lately."

"Well," Leslie said. "I decided that it's fun to break a few rules, but I can't completely blow my grades. So I've made myself a promise to get back to the books and slow down with Nathan—at least until exams are over." She shook her head, then laughed. "It sure won't be easy."

"I guess not," Bess said. "Nathan's pretty cute."

Leslie nodded. "Yes. But I've worked too hard to wreck everything now."

"Well, I'm just glad you're okay. I was kind of worried," Bess said.

"Never again. Next time I stay out all night, I'll try to remember to give you a call, or whatever."

Bess thumped her pillow. "Deal. And by the way, I've learned something from all this: that it must be a real pain to have a complete slob like me for a roommate. I hereby resolve to be neater from now on!"

Nancy sipped tea from a delicate bone china cup and studied Leila Vandenbrock while she talked about Lauren. There was no denying the resemblance to her famous sister—those exquisite eyes, the famous widow's peak. Yet as Nancy looked closer, she could see that there were subtle differences. For one thing, Leila's mouth was thinner, and there had been a vibrancy about Lauren that was missing from Leila.

"People used to mistake us for twins when we were children," Mrs. Vandenbrock was saying, staring mistily into the blazing fire. "But

we were very different. Lauren was the more
spirited. She was like a pacing tiger. She
couldn't wait to break out of our small town
and make her mark on Hollywood. Or fall in
love. I got married first, but my marriage was
already breaking up when my sister came to
join me in Chicago.

"Lauren and I lived together for about a
year. And then I met Wendell, and my life
changed overnight." Mrs. Vandenbrock smiled
and Nancy saw that a warm, gentle glow lit her
face when she talked about him. "He was the
most romantic man I had ever met. We had a
mad, whirlwind courtship, and were married
within six months. But nothing would persuade
Lauren to move back with us to Wendell's
hometown of Weston. She'd been hounded
enough by the American press, she said, and
she just wanted to get away somewhere. She
felt tortured about leaving her baby son."

"So what happened then?" Nancy prodded
gently, wanting to hear more about Lauren.

"Wendell was so understanding and generous. He sent her to Europe, and he bought her
a small house in the mountains of France. She
lived there until her death from cancer, three
years ago," Mrs. Vandenbrock said. Then she
paused and gave Nancy a measured glance.

"I tried to get her to contact Sean those last
few years, especially after his father died,"
Mrs. Vandenbrock added. "But Lauren was

convinced she'd be rejected. And she couldn't bear any more pain, she told me."

Nancy set her cup in its saucer. "I don't understand why Mrs. Fletcher left her son in the first place if it was so painful."

Leila Vandenbrock's face tightened. "It's not because Lauren murdered Jacobs, if that's what you were thinking. She did have an affair with Jacobs, that much is true. But my sister was not a murderer."

Nancy sat silently, waiting for Mrs. Vandenbrock to go on.

"Everyone who knew Lauren loved her. She was happy and the life of the party, and she'd never hurt anyone," Mrs. Vandenbrock declared. "She went over to Jacobs's house the morning of the last day of filming, because Jacobs had asked her to come over to talk about their affair—"

"But I heard that Jacobs broke off the affair with Mrs. Fletcher, and that was what made her so upset," Nancy cut in.

Mrs. Vandenbrock shook her head. "No," she said angrily. "Of course, that was what was churning around the rumor mill in Hollywood. But it wasn't the truth. Lauren was trying to save her marriage for Sean's sake. But Jacobs wanted to resume the affair. He was in love with my sister. Lauren agreed to meet him only because she wanted to convince him once and for all that it was over."

The butler knocked and entered, and Mrs. Vandenbrock was silent while he quickly removed the tea things. She continued with her story after he left the library.

"Lauren told me that when she got to his house, she found him dead," Mrs. Vandenbrock explained. "It was clear that there'd been a struggle—an overturned chair, some broken glass, and a gun on the floor. And there was something else, small—like a shoelace . . ." Leila frowned, then shook her head. "I can't remember, my memory fails me.

"Anyway, Lauren wasn't thinking straight, as you might guess. She was hysterical and foolishly picked up the gun, then dropped it. In a panic she called Sebastian, who told her not to touch anything else before he got there."

"I'm sure she was terrified," Nancy said, her head swimming with images. The decades-old drama seemed to be playing out right before her.

Mrs. Vandenbrock went on. "But when Sebastian got there, he made it clear that he thought *she* did it. Lauren tried to tell him she was innocent, but he didn't believe her. Then he said he'd make a deal. He'd take care of everything and make Jacobs's death look like a suicide. But in return he wanted a divorce from Lauren—and full custody of Sean.

Lauren was to leave town and never contact Sean again."

"That was pretty harsh," Nancy murmured.

Mrs. Vandenbrock nodded grimly. "This was a man acting out of pain and rage over the affair. Sebastian told Lauren that she could take it or leave it, but if she didn't accept his terms, he'd sit back and let her go to jail. He gave her all of thirty seconds to make up her mind. Lauren was scared, confused. She wasn't thinking straight. She felt she had no choice, so she took the deal.

"Then, Sebastian told her to collect herself and go back to the set, to pretend that everything was normal."

Nancy said, "Talk about a test of acting talents. She must have been overwhelmed."

"Well, it wasn't easy," Leila said. "Lauren managed to force herself through the filming that day when they were shooting the alternate ending scene. Sebastian showed up an hour later. Jacobs's body was found by one of his assistants that night, and Lauren never knew who really committed the murder," Mrs. Vandenbrock finished.

Nancy's mind was filled with questions. If it wasn't a suicide, and Lauren didn't kill him, then who murdered David Jacobs?

CHAPTER 12

Casey was sitting across from Erika Swann in Java Joe's. They had just finished an early supper, and were now sipping coffees while they waited for Terry and Sean to meet them for the final screening of the Sebastian Fletcher film festival.

Erika's glamorous presence had caused a stir from the moment she'd entered the popular campus hangout. It didn't matter that she was dressed casually in a thick gray woolen sweater and pants. Her obvious elegance and star quality still shone through. Several students had stopped by their booth and, holding out Java Joe's napkins, had asked for Erika's autograph. She obliged graciously, obviously pleased to be recognized. Casey was glad Erika appeared to be having a good time.

"Are you enjoying your visit?" Casey asked Erika.

Erika smiled. "Oh, yes. Everyone at Wilder's gone out of their way to be nice. And I haven't seen Rob Delucca in years. We went to dinner and got caught up on each other's projects."

"I'm glad this visit is turning out to be fun for you," Casey said.

Erika smiled at Casey. "How about you? That looks like an engagement ring you're wearing."

Casey held up her diamond so Erika could get a closer look. "Charley Stern and I just got engaged. But we're not getting married until after I finish college."

Erika nodded. "School and settling down with one guy. All of this must seem tame to you after your success in *The President's Daughter*. Do you ever miss the excitement?" she asked.

"Oh, not much," Casey replied. "It's not like I don't have plenty of excitement here at Wilder."

Suddenly Casey remembered what she'd promised Nancy. "And I still keep in touch with my friends in Hollywood," Casey told Erika. "In fact, wait till I tell you what's been going on lately."

While they finished drinking their coffees, Casey explained to Erika about Nancy's theory regarding Mrs. Vandenbrock.

"Don't you think it's exciting?" Casey

asked, trying to draw a response from Erika. She'd been curiously silent while Casey told the story.

Erika sipped her coffee. "Very exciting," she said dryly. Her luminous eyes were dark and unfathomable.

That's odd, Casey thought to herself. You'd think Erika would be thrilled for Sean. After all, they are colleagues.

Casey studied the older woman, trying to figure her out. "Do you think Lauren did it?" Casey asked, leaning closer so that she wouldn't be overheard.

Erika shifted in her seat and again lifted her mug to her lips. "That's hard," she said. "I liked Lauren, and I thoroughly enjoyed working with her. I don't want to think that she killed Jacobs, but I just can't believe he committed suicide either. Even if he was upset that their affair ended, it just doesn't seem like he'd resort to something as drastic—so permanent—as suicide."

Casey nodded, but then she thought about something Erika had said. "Don't some people think *he* was the one to end the affair?"

Erika frowned. "Well, yes. But it still must have been such a muddle."

Casey looked up as she saw Terry heading toward their booth. "Here comes Terry now," she said, somewhat disappointed that she couldn't continue drawing Erika out. Oh well, it hadn't been going all that well.

"Hello," he replied, smiling broadly. "So, what do you think of Java Joe's?"

"Very nice," Erika said. She did a quick check in her mini-compact, reapplied her lipstick, and flashed her million-dollar smile at Terry. "It's so charming of you to come for us," she added.

Casey smiled to herself. What a flirt the older woman could be. Oh, well, that's the entertainment business. Never age—and always play to your audience. She glanced behind Terry, but didn't see Sean.

"Where's Sean?" Casey hoped she didn't sound too eager, but she'd looked forward to seeing him. And I'm not being disloyal to Charley, she told herself firmly.

Terry held his palms up and shrugged. "I have no idea. I was going to ask if you'd seen him," he said.

"No," Casey said. She was baffled. "Did you call his hotel?"

"I did. This morning," Terry said. "But he wasn't there. I thought it kind of odd. I mean, where would he go? He's already taken a tour of the campus, and Weston's not exactly the kind of happening place where a well-known actor would want to go sightseeing."

"Well, who knows?" Casey said excitedly. "Weston might be happening for Sean in a way we never imagined. Maybe he's with his mother at this very moment!"

Jake sat at Nancy's desk and listened while she told him the incredible tale of Sean and his mother.

"And so it turns out that Leila Vandenbrock is his aunt," Nancy said. "His mother died three years ago, without ever contacting Sean. It's such a tragedy. But at least now Sean knows what became of her, and he can begin to put some questions to rest."

"Sounds like this will make for a pretty interesting final screening," Jake said, absorbing what he'd just heard. He studied Nancy for a moment. You just never knew with her, he thought. Here all this time, he'd been wondering if she cared about him as much as he'd thought. And, of course, she cared. It was simply that Nancy couldn't help getting caught up in a mystery.

Jake smiled. Nancy looked great right then. But then, to him, she always looked great. She was wearing a black satiny vest over an ivory blouse and tight jeans. Her lips were glossed over with a creamy red lipstick. Once again Jake found himself noticing how kissable those lips were.

"Are you sure you have to go to this screening?" Jake asked.

Nancy kissed him lightly on the lips. "Yes,

I do." She slipped her hand into his. "But I'm glad you're coming along."

"Good," Jake said. "And though I wouldn't mind staying here and kissing you some more, I am actually intrigued by this whole thing and—if you can believe it—I'm also interested in seeing this film. Which, I might add, we're going to be late for if we don't hurry."

Nancy rooted through her closet and emerged with her black wool blazer. "Now, where's my hair clip? I'm sorry to keep you waiting. I'm almost ready—just got a late start. That's what happens when you get caught up in a great story."

While Jake waited for Nancy to finish getting ready, his journalist's brain kicked into gear. This was some story, he thought. An article for the *Wilder Times*? Another shared by-line for the two of us? He turned over several possibilities in his mind.

"I'm glad I could talk you into coming," Nancy said.

Jake looked up. "Thanks for taking a chance and inviting me to another screening," he said. "I figured it was high time I saw for myself what was up with this Sebastian Fletcher and his films."

And, he admitted to himself, because he wanted to get a closer look at Terry Schneider, who seemed to be receiving a great deal of Nancy's attention lately. Should he be worried? Jake wondered. He supposed Nancy might think Terry was good-looking, but still, Jake thought, Terry didn't really seem like Nancy's type. I'm her type, he told himself firmly.

"Now there's only one thing bothering me," Nancy said, turning to face Jake.

"Huh?" Jake said, emerging from his daydreaming. It was hard keeping up with the way Nancy's mind worked.

Nancy didn't appear to notice that he'd been distracted. She said, "I still haven't figured out who killed Jacobs."

Jake crossed the room to sit on Nancy's bed. "Maybe no one killed him," he said. "He might really have committed suicide."

"No, I disagree," Nancy said. "Someone had been in the room fighting with Jacobs. Mrs. Vandenbrock distinctly said that Lauren mentioned there were signs of a struggle."

"What kind of a struggle?"

"She said that there were overturned chairs and broken glass and some other object that she couldn't remember—a shoestring or something."

"I wonder what that was," Jake mused. "That could be a clue."

Nancy nodded. "That's what I've been thinking." She said as she picked the publicity photo up off her desk. Nancy went over to the bed and sat down next to Jake.

Jake reached over to brush her hair off her neck and leaned in closer, pressing a few kisses on her neck. Nancy smiled and started to respond.

Suddenly she sat up straight. "Hey, wait! Look at this," Nancy exclaimed, holding the photo in front of his face so that he was forced to stop kissing her.

"What?" he asked, trying to conceal his disappointment. Jake wanted to have Nancy melt into his arms and stay there permanently. He didn't really want to think about Jacobs and his mysterious death.

"There's something about this photo that bothers me," Nancy said. "Something isn't right."

Jake gave up on kissing her and studied the photo closely. "Well, the clothes and jewelry, for one thing. Talk about weird getups," he said after a moment. "Those necklaces. They're huge. They look like they could choke a person."

"Hmmm." Suddenly Nancy snapped her fingers. "Of course. That's it," she said.

With that, she leaped up and went over to Kara's dresser, where she started rummaging through the tangle of jewelry on the top.

"Look at all this stuff," she muttered. "How can Kara ever find anything in this mess?"

After a moment, she pounced on something.

"Voilà!" she exclaimed, holding up the replica of the necklace Erika Swann's character wore.

"Voilà, what?" Jake asked.

"See this pendant?" Nancy pointed to the large object hanging from the leather cord.

Jake was confused. He didn't see what she was getting at. "Yeah. So what's the big deal?"

"So the big deal is that in the movie, her pendant is on a black leather thong. But in this photo, the necklace is on a piece of black satin ribbon," Nancy said triumphantly. "You can see that it's flat and wider than the leather would be."

"Like I said, so?" Jake asked. He was starting to get annoyed. Enough was enough.

Nancy went on excitedly. "The ribbon is wrong. The pendant should be on a leather thong, like in the movie. The character even has a line about how the leather gets too tight around her throat after she gets the necklace wet in a swimming scene and it shrinks." Nancy paused a minute before continuing.

"Were there two necklaces or did someone lose the leather piece? Now the question is, when was this publicity photo taken?"

Jake realized that Nancy was lost in thought as her conversation stopped and she stared at the photo. Suddenly she got up and reached for the phone, punching in numbers as fast as she could.

"Who are you calling?" Jake asked. This

was getting weirder by the minute. "Would you mind filling me in a little here?"

Nancy hung up, and she appeared not to have even heard Jake's question. "She's not there." With that, she grabbed her purse then pulled at Jake's arm. "Come on. I want to get over to Hewlitt."

"Okay, whatever you say," Jake said, shaking his head as he followed Nancy out of her room.

What was she up to now? he wondered.

"Wow," Casey said, gazing at Sean after he'd finished telling his story to the small seated group assembled around him in Hewlitt's lobby. She glanced at the faces of the others, wanting to see their reactions to the dramatic tale.

Terry looked amazed, and Leila Vandenbrock terribly sad. Erika Swann and Rob Delucca, Casey was surprised to note, simply acted uncomfortable. The whole group was quiet amid the excitement of last-minute preparations for the final screening of the Sebastian Fletcher film festival.

"Well, there it is," Sean said, the soft lobby lights playing off his handsome face. "The end of a long search. It's hard to accept that I will never have a chance to get to know my mother. But the good news is that I've been lucky in another way."

He smiled warmly at Leila Vandenbrock, who was sitting on the sofa next to him. "I have found someone very important, my aunt."

Poor Sean, Casey thought. All those years of searching for his mother and to have it end like this. Still, finding an aunt you never knew you had was pretty special. When Casey looked at Leila Vandenbrock, it was obvious to her that Mrs. Vandenbrock was also happy to have connected with Sean at last.

However, Casey sensed that Mrs. Vandenbrock wasn't fond of Erika and Rob. Her manner was distant and formal with them. Mrs. Vandenbrock was even a bit frosty to Casey after someone told her about Casey's TV career. To Casey, it seemed as though Mrs. Vandenbrock held anyone associated with Hollywood and the film world responsible for her sister's tragedy.

Casey's gaze rested again on Erika and Rob. They hadn't spoken much this evening, Casey mused. As a matter of fact, they both looked distinctly uncomfortable, Erika toying with a tassel on her purse, and Rob looking over everyone's heads as if he wished he were someplace else.

Did they know something about the murder? What if one of them was the murderer? Casey couldn't help thinking. Rob could have had some beef with Jacobs. But Erika? Casey wondered if the sweet woman she knew could be a cold-blooded killer.

The next minute Casey admonished herself. Chill a little. You're going off the deep end. You're getting too carried away with this tragic story and starting to imagine everyone around is involved with it.

"What time are we going to start?" Rob asked, looking at his watch.

Terry jumped to his feet. "Whoa. I'm sorry. I guess I got caught up in all this."

He looked around at the small group. "We're scheduled to watch *Candlelight Vigil* as the last film. But since I promised we'd watch that reel of outtakes from *Road to Nowhere*, we'll start tonight by watching the outtakes, then see the film. Okay?"

The rest of the group agreed. Erika and Rob drifted off to talk with several filmgoers who were clamoring for their attention. Casey went to the refreshment table and poured herself a cup of coffee. She studied Rob and Erika some more, then turned her attention to the activity around her. Nancy and Jake were just arriving and greeting Leila Vandenbrock.

When it was time to fill the theater, Casey followed Nancy, Jake, and Mrs. Vandenbrock down the center aisle to take their seats. Terry announced the program change, and the audience waited as the projectionist put in the reel of outtakes.

While the theater continued filling up with stragglers, Casey made herself comfortable and people watched. It was then she became aware that Nancy and Jake were in deep conversation with Mrs. Vandenbrock, talking earnestly about something.

Nancy seems so intense, Casey thought to herself. I wonder what's going on?

CHAPTER 13

"Mrs. Vandenbrock, tell me again about how Lauren described the murder scene," Nancy said to the older woman as they waited for the outtake reel to start. "I'm sorry to keep pressing the issue, but I'm curious."

"What else is there to tell?" Leila Vandenbrock asked. "I've already told you everything I know."

"You mentioned that there was an object next to David Jacobs's body," Nancy said, trying not to get too excited. "You thought your sister said it might have been a shoelace. Could it possibly have been a thin strip of leather?"

Mrs. Vandenbrock pursed her lips. "Now that you've reminded me, that is what Lauren described." She looked at Nancy sharply. "How did you know?"

Nancy felt her heart start beating faster. She

was getting somewhere, she thought. "It was just a hunch," she said.

"Lauren didn't go into any detail," Mrs. Vandenbrock said. "What's so important about a leather shoelace?"

But just as Nancy started to answer, the lights dimmed and the outtake reel began. The first outtake was of a swimming pool scene. The camera zoomed in on Lauren's character just getting out of the water. The man standing next to her on the deck started his lines, only suddenly, he was seized by a fit of loud hiccups. Lauren was trying not to break character, but finally couldn't contain herself. Several members of the audience roared and clapped.

Soon the theater was filled with the sounds of laughter as the hilarious outtakes rolled on. But funny as they were, Nancy didn't join in the laughter. She was lost in thought.

A piece of leather on the ground, she thought to herself. Publicity photos of Erika's character with ribbon instead of leather holding the pendant. Were there two necklaces?

Nancy's mind raced on. Was Erika with Jacobs that day? And what if she were? It made absolutely no sense. Why would Erika kill him?

Someone else, then. Maybe someone with access to the costumes? Could it be Rob? But why? Nancy chewed on that for a few minutes while the laughter echoed around her in the darkened theater.

She glanced over to where Rob was sitting. He looked nothing like a murderer, but he did act very uncomfortable whenever the scandal was brought up.

Nancy's attention was dragged back to the screen as Erika's image filled the theater. It was an outtake of Erika flubbing the same line over and over.

"Oh, no. Not this one. Do you *have* to show it?" Erika called out in mock horror, and the audience laughed louder than ever.

Suddenly Nancy noticed something on the screen. She looked closer. Erika's pendant necklace was hanging from a piece of black satin ribbon, just like in the publicity photo.

"Now wait a minute," Nancy said, half out loud. Is this an outtake from the reshot ending, done after Jacobs died?

Blinding light filled the theater as the reel ended. The audience applauded wildly and wolf whistled while Terry walked up to the stage.

"On behalf of the Focus Film Society, I hope you enjoyed seeing some of those memorable moments," he said after the clapping subsided. "And now we'd like to take a short break before we show our final film."

Ginny set her highlighter down and looked up from her notebook at the Beat Poets as they practiced in their garage rehearsal space.

She closed her eyes to rest them from reading so much and listened to the sounds of the band.

How much longer could this rehearsal go? Ginny wondered. She'd been sitting and studying for what seemed like hours. As far as she was concerned, the band sounded fine. They didn't need to make a marathon session out of this. Finally the sounds died away.

"I can't get over it. Just think, with all those flights back and forth to Los Angeles, we'll be frequent flyers," Ray said to the other guys when they paused for a break.

"And we'll probably go on tour later," added Bruce, the drummer. He twirled some drumsticks between his fingers. "Can you see us wearing black satin baseball jackets that say, The Beat Poets—World Tour?"

Ginny couldn't help smiling at their enthusiasm, but at the same time, she worried about Ray. He was so busy rehearsing that he wasn't studying much these days. And with exam week coming up shortly, she knew it could spell disaster for his grades. Especially biology, his weakest subject.

Thinking about it, Ginny felt the old resentment building up within her. Over the past few weeks she'd spent hours helping Ray study. He'd been getting terrific grades. Now all that effort would be wasted.

When the other band members disappeared

outside for their break, Ginny got up and walked over to where Ray was setting down his guitar.

"Hi, babe," Ray said. "How do we sound?"

"Great," Ginny said. Then after a pause she added, "Ray, I know this is thrilling, and I couldn't be happier about your recording contract, but couldn't you study some now and practice more later?" she asked.

Ray put his arm around her. "Aw, Ginny, don't worry about me," he said affectionately. "I've got my priorities straight. I'm going to study as soon as we go over a few more pieces."

Ginny hated to enter the nag zone, but she was feeling more and more uneasy. She looked up as Spider came back into the garage, brandishing a soda for Ray. "Promise?" she asked.

Ray kissed her on the top of her head and took the soda from Spider. "I promise," he said lightly to Ginny. Then he turned back to his band. "All right, everyone. Amp it up. Let's take it from the top."

The sounds started up again, and Ginny wandered back to the overturned milk crates where her books awaited. As the energetic strains of music reached her ears, Ginny thought about frequent flying and world tours and sighed. This record business was exciting all right. But for the first time, it occurred to Ginny that while it was an incredible opportunity, it was much more complicated than it seemed at first. Being under contract with a major record company was going to take a lot of time and a serious reshifting of priorities. Ray was going to have his hands full balancing all the separate aspects of his life.

Terry headed up the aisle to make his way toward the crowded refreshment table in the lobby. People congratulated him, and he smiled in response. He was beginning to feel the strain of putting together a film festival. It had been a lot of fun but also a great deal of work. There was no doubt that it was a complete success, but now he was tired.

"Just what I need," he said to the guy working the coffee machine.

After he poured some cream into his steaming cup, he scanned the crowd for Nancy. He only saw Jake approaching the coffee table.

Nancy's boyfriend, Terry thought, furrowing his brow. Terry studied him for a moment. On impulse, he decided to go over and talk with him.

"Jake. Glad you could come tonight," Terry said. He wondered just how close Jake and Nancy were. She was a very attractive woman. If this wasn't a serious relationship, maybe he'd ask Nancy out.

"Great show," Jake said. "Those outtakes

were something, weren't they? I haven't laughed so much in a long time."

Terry nodded, sipping his coffee. "Amazing what goes on behind the scenes, things that people never imagined."

Just then he saw Nancy across the room talking with Sean. She was standing inches away from him, her head tilted up so that her hair fanned out around her shoulders. Terry glanced at Jake and saw that Jake's eyes were trained on Nancy.

"Nancy's really terrific, isn't she," Terry said.

Jake nodded. "She is. We've gotten to know each other pretty well lately. We spend quite a lot of time working together on the *Wilder Times,* and socially as well. She's a good person, and she has a real flair for journalism."

"Oh, so you're pretty tight, then, huh?" Terry asked.

Jake rubbed his strong jaw. "I think that would be accurate."

Terry didn't miss the unspoken message in Jake's words. Well, that settles that, he thought. It's clear that Nancy is taken.

"Hi, Jake. Hi, Terry."

Terry nodded at Casey as she appeared in front of them. Casey was wearing a stylish, blue silk blouse that complemented her short red hair. Terry found himself studying her perfect features. No wonder she had been a star. Casey was very attractive.

"Have you seen Erika?" she asked, giving him a blast of her famous smile.

Casey sure is a looker, Terry thought while he shook his head in answer to her question. But then his eye traveled to the diamond she was wearing on her left hand. In the next minute he was laughing at himself.

How *do* you manage it, Schneider? he thought. Just your luck to be attracted to two unavailable women in the same week!

Nancy waved as she approached Sean in the lobby and waited patiently while several people pestered him for his autograph.

"Hi, Nancy," he said, brightening when he saw her.

"Do you ever mind giving autographs?" she asked Sean conversationally when they moved away.

Sean shook his head. "Not really. It's all part of the business."

Nancy nodded, then took a deep breath to ask her next question. "I wanted to know something about the outtakes we just saw. Were they from the original ending or the alternate ending?"

"From the alternate ending," he said. "I remember my dad saying there were so many mistakes that day. I suppose it would be natural considering how exhausted everyone must have been from filming."

"You're right, everyone was exhausted," Erika said as she drifted over with Casey and Rob.

"Well, I have something else I'm curious about." This time Nancy directed her question to Rob. She rummaged through her handbag and pulled out the publicity photo. "When was this photo taken?" she asked the art director.

Rob studied the photo for a moment. "At the end of the last day," he said. "I remember how upset the publicity woman was because David Jacobs wasn't there to supervise the shoot. He'd been very specific about wanting to choose the set-up scenes for the photos."

"I see," said Nancy, her mind racing. "What happened then?"

"The cast was told to wait, and they were complaining because they wanted to finish filming," explained Rob. "But finally Sebastian arrived, and he insisted on supervising the photo shoot so they could get on with the filming.

"Of course, none of us had any idea what had happened to Jacobs."

At that point Nancy saw Sean shoot her a puzzled glance. "I don't get it," exclaimed Sean. "What's with all the questions?"

Nancy was silent for a moment. "Because I think I know who killed David Jacobs."

With that, she turned to Erika. "You did, didn't you?"

"I beg your pardon!" Erika's eyes flashed. "How dare you!"

Casey stepped in. "Nancy!" she said in a horrified voice.

Nancy held up the photo and pointed to the changed necklace. "This is a different necklace, isn't it?" she asked Erika quietly. "You lost the real necklace—the leather thong—during your struggle with David Jacobs. I'll bet that the police report makes mention of a leather thong found at the murder scene."

"I don't know what you're talking about!"

"I think you do," Nancy said steadily.

Erika regarded Nancy without blinking or looking away, as if sizing her up.

"This is outrageous," Erika said, but her voice didn't carry the conviction of her words.

Nancy continued staring Erika down. After a moment Erika reached for her throat, dropped her hand to her side, and appeared to go limp. She suddenly looked older and resigned.

"I'm so tired of all the hiding and the lies. Always worried and waiting for someone to discover the truth," Erika said, almost in a whisper. She turned her exquisite eyes on Sean.

"You have no idea of how hard it's been to carry this around with me all these years. I knew this day would finally come. Yes, I killed David Jacobs."

She started crying, dabbing at the moisture gathering in the corners of her eyes. Nancy saw how stunned and upset Rob appeared. She also noticed that Sean appeared to be unmoved. His handsome face was now stony and cold.

"I'm so sorry," Erika said. She reached out to touch Sean on the shoulder, but he jerked away.

"You were my friend," he said in a chilly voice. "I played at your house when I was a little kid. You threw birthday parties for me. You let me drive your car when I got my learner's permit. I used to talk to you about my mother. And the whole time, it was *you* who killed Jacobs, who caused all this pain? I want to know why."

Erika looked down. "It's a long story—" she said tiredly.

"Don't worry," Nancy cut in. "You'll have plenty of time to tell the police."

Erika didn't even flinch when Nancy turned to go to the pay phone.

CHAPTER 14

Eileen was balancing her book bag and fumbling at her room door with her key. The sun had long ago ducked behind the university buildings, and in the semidarkness it was hard for Eileen to find the lock. She didn't notice the small cream-colored envelope until she opened the door and it fluttered to the floor.

"What's this?" Eileen asked, picking it up as she entered her room. Her name was written in unfamiliar, bold handwriting across the envelope. Frowning, she turned it over.

Wonder who it's from, she thought.

Once in her room Eileen dumped her book bag on her bed and sat down. She was exhausted. She hadn't slept much the previous night, and she'd spent the entire day studying in the Rock. If she were honest with herself, she'd admit that she'd gone there as much to hide out as to study.

The Rock had been a quiet refuge for Eileen. Locked away in a study carrel near the stacks, Eileen had felt safe. She could lose herself in her studies and not have to think about her disastrous date with Emmet. She didn't have to remember the way he'd looked at her when she'd made cracks about brainless jocks or any of the other thoughtless remarks she'd made.

It was only on her way back to her dorm room that she'd begun to think about Emmet at all. And the weird thing was, when she thought about him, she couldn't quite conjure up the anger she'd felt when he'd spilled his coffee on her dress.

Instead, she found herself wondering what was really going on behind those handsome eyes of his. What it might feel like to run her hands through his thick sandy hair, to be taken up in his strong, athletic arms? Of course, that would mean she'd have to stop waging war with him and really get to know Emmet.

So stupid! Eileen said to herself. Talk about ridiculous. It wasn't even worth pursuing. She'd been right to tell her friends that she'd given up on dating. She just wasn't cut out for it. And she and Emmet were probably the worst dating combination ever. They were just too different. They clashed too much.

"Let's face it," Eileen said. "We can't be in the same room without infuriating each other."

Looking at the envelope, Eileen traced over her name. Finally she tore it open and took out a small card. Pasted on the card was a white flag made out of a tiny square of torn cotton. Someone had drawn in a thin, wobbly flagpole.

"Let's call a truce." Eileen read the words on the card. "Can we try again? How about at the pep rally for next week's football game? Call me: 555-1435." Eileen looked at the name scrawled in that same bold handwriting at the bottom: Emmet.

Eileen was surprised at the happiness that took hold of her. She reread the card and traced her finger over the little white flag. Who'd have thought Emmet would go to so much trouble and make up a card? She glanced over at the phone. It would be so easy to pick up the phone, make the call, listen to Emmet's voice, and then say yes. Eileen took a deep breath and lifted up the receiver. Her fingers didn't even tremble as she punched in the numbers.

"Hello, Emmet? It's Eileen," she said as soon as she heard his deep, resonating voice. "I got your card, and I have one question for you: Are you sure you know what you're doing?"

Emmet chuckled. "No."

"Pardon me?" Eileen gasped. Was this a joke?

"No," Emmet said. "I'm not sure at all. But the way I see it, life's all about taking chances, isn't it?"

"I don't know," Eileen said uncertainly, clutching the phone.

"Are you up for the challenge?" Emmet asked.

Eileen smiled. "Okay, why not? Works for me. You're on!"

Casey was sitting cross-legged across from Terry in the lounge of Suite 301. They both jumped up as Nancy came through the door.

"So what happened? You've been at the police station for hours," Casey practically shouted. "I've been going absolutely out of my mind waiting and wondering."

Nancy dropped her purse onto the sofa and shrugged off her jacket.

"It was something, all right," Nancy said as she took a seat. "After Sean and Rob and I got down to the station, we had to wait forever while Erika talked to the police, and they spoke with the authorities out in California. Finally we found out the whole story, and it isn't what any of us could have guessed."

Nancy went on. "Turns out that *Erika* and Jacobs had a very secret, very short fling while *Road to Nowhere* was being filmed, after Lauren had broken it off with Jacobs."

"No way!" Casey gasped. "Erika Swann? An affair with Jacobs?"

Nancy nodded. "But Jacobs didn't want to pursue a relationship with Erika because he was obsessed with Lauren. He told Erika that he didn't want to see her again."

Casey's eyes widened. "How did Erika take it?"

"Not very well," Nancy said. "She was crazy about him, so she became desperate. She was young and foolish—her own words. She wanted Jacobs to love her."

"This whole thing just doesn't stop surprising anyone," Terry said, shaking his head.

"You said it," Nancy said. "On the last day of filming, Erika went to his house to try to convince him to come back to her, but Jacobs just laughed at her and told her to get out. Erika went into a rage. She couldn't bear being mocked like that. She slapped him, and then Jacobs went ballistic. He apparently lunged at her and pulled off her necklace, trying to get at her throat. I guess the prop necklace wasn't on very securely."

Nancy took a deep breath. "Anyway, Jacobs backed off," she said. "But then he came at her again, and they struggled some more. Erika says she was certain he meant to really hurt her, so she looked around for something else to defend herself with.

Jacobs owned a gun, and he had it out on

the desk. She grabbed for it. Erika swears the gun went off as they were struggling. Then, in a panic, she ran from the scene."

"So it was Erika the whole time. Poor Lauren," Casey said softly. She felt a fresh wave of sympathy for all that Lauren and Sean had been through. There had been so many years of lies and secrets.

"Erika went back to the set and tried to act as if nothing had happened," Nancy continued. "But she was late for wardrobe and then realized that they were going to shoot the publicity stills before they finished filming. She wasn't thinking clearly and grabbed another pendant necklace that they'd used in early rehearsals. This one had the pendant hanging from a black satin ribbon, not black leather."

"She must have figured that she'd be arrested any minute because her fingerprints were on the gun," Terry said thoughtfully.

"That's right," Nancy said. "So she was pretty shocked that night when she saw on the news that Jacobs had been found dead, and the authorities were calling it an apparent suicide, because Jacobs was found with the gun in his hand. She realized someone must have been to the murder scene after her. When she heard the rumors about Lauren, Erika figured it probably was Sebastian or Lauren."

"What a coward," Terry said. "How could

she have lived with herself all those years knowing what she knew?"

"I guess she didn't care," Casey said. "She was just so glad to have saved her own neck, she never gave any thought to how the whole thing affected anyone else's life."

"Obviously not," Nancy said reflectively. "She probably didn't think about anything but not being found out."

"What will happen to Erika now?" Casey asked.

"For starters, she'll be taken back to Los Angeles, and then who knows," Nancy answered. "She's waived her rights and confessed. But I'm sure she'll get some high-priced lawyer. I suppose she could claim self-defense."

Terry furrowed his brow. "But if that were so, she might have gotten off easy if she'd told the truth long ago."

"It's too bad, isn't it, that Sebastian's anger at his wife hurt his son?" Nancy said. "And that Lauren didn't have the courage to see Sean again before she died. Sean was so desperate to know his mother. Mrs. V. showed Sean a scrapbook that Lauren kept over the years of every newspaper or magazine article she could find about him."

"That's so awful," Casey said, her eyes filling with tears.

"What about Sean and Leila?" Terry asked.

"Sean is going to Europe with Mrs. Vandenbrock to find his mother's grave. At least he'll get to know his mother somewhat through Mrs. V."

Casey nodded. "They already seem to be fond of each other.

Nancy stood up and ran her hands through her hair. "What a day, huh?" she asked. "And now I've got to get going. I have to meet Jake."

"I need to be somewhere too," Terry said abruptly, and he stood up to follow Nancy out.

After they left Casey sat for a while, drumming her fingers on the armrest of the sofa and thinking about love and betrayal and the way it shaped people's lives. It was ironic, she mused, that there was more drama behind the scenes in Hollywood than had ever been captured on film.

Suddenly she felt a powerful urge to hear Charley's voice. She picked up the phone and punched in his number.

Stephanie pressed the elevator buttons, and while she waited, she fluffed her hair. If only she didn't have to work today, she thought. It was beyond depressing. She didn't know if she could face the toy department again or the grubby little customers.

When Stephanie got to her floor, she started over toward the toy department. She was about to place her purse in the cabinet under the cash register, when Mr. Barnwell darted in front of her, blocking her path.

"You'vebeentransferred," he said quickly, his words running together the way they often did. His bespectacled eyes glinted with obvious satisfaction. "No use trying to talk me out of it. I just can't have someone with an attitude like yours in my department."

That's because you're such a hopeless nerd, and I'm simply too cool for you, Stephanie wanted to say. But instead, she gave him an icy look and examined a chip in her nail polish. "Thank goodness. So where am I supposed to go?"

"You've been assigned to cosmetics." With that, Mr. Barnwell turned away to arrange a display of dolls.

"Have fun playing with your toys," Stephanie said nastily to Mr. Barnwell.

Stephanie laughed as Mr. Barnwell blushed. Then she sauntered toward the elevator. Actually, cosmetics sounded about as good as anything at Berrigan's. Then she remembered that cosmetics was the department where Pam Miller worked.

Just as long as she doesn't think this means we're going to be buddy-buddy now, Stephanie told herself. Well, she'd simply have to ignore Pam and Pam would get the message.

A thought struck her as the elevator bell

sounded and the doors opened, and she recalled what Pam had said about all the free samples she got. Perfume, makeup, lipstick, nail polish. Okay, if she got first crack at some decent samples, maybe, she decided, she could get used to wearing a smock. Stephanie walked faster. She slowed just before approaching the counters.

"I wonder what kind of overly made-up, poufy-haired supervisor I'll get this time," she said under her breath. "Every time I switch departments, the supervisors get worse and worse."

"You must be the new salesclerk for cosmetics." A full, rich voice cut into her thoughts.

Stephanie looked over her shoulder. It was none other than the gorgeous Jonathan Baur. As usual, he was dressed in a wonderfully tailored suit, and Stephanie did a double-take.

"Well, yes, I am," she said. Then she gave Jonathan a wide smile.

"Your supervisor, Ms. McKelvy, is in a meeting now. She'll be here shortly to orient you to your new department. I'm the floor manager," Jonathan said. "And I'd like to start off by saying that I've heard a lot of complaints about you. If you're interested in lasting for any length of time at Berrigan's, you're going to have to drop the attitude. Understand?"

Stephanie looked into Jonathan's dark, mysterious eyes. He looked particularly handsome when he was trying to be stern. She couldn't wait to see what he'd look like when she made him want her. Starting now, she'd get to work on him. Was this her lucky day, or what?

"Anything you say, Boss," she purred. "Anything you say."

Nancy had just knocked on Jake's apartment door.

I hope he's home, she thought. After all, she finally had a few minutes to see him and it would be too disappointing if she missed another chance to spend time with him.

At last she heard footsteps and was relieved when Jake opened the door. He was wearing a deep forest green sweater that made the most of his gorgeous eyes.

"Nancy, what brings you to this neck of the woods," Jake asked.

Nancy stepped inside his apartment. "Big news," she said. "Erika told the police everything about her involvement in Jacob's death—and I've gotten a great journalism profile as well," she said.

Jake motioned for her to sit in a chair at his kitchen table, and she did.

"Way to go," Jake said. "Tell all."

Nancy hurriedly filled in the pieces of the story. "So what do you think?"

Jake examined a spot on his cowboy boots for a minute before asking, "I think, wow, as

I always do. You're an incredible woman, Nancy."

"Thanks," Nancy said, feeling warm with Jake's praise. "It's nice to be able to help when you can. But what do you think of the story?"

Jake smiled. "It's all pretty amazing. Who'd have guessed it would turn out this way?"

"Definitely not me," Nancy said with a laugh. "I was beginning to believe I'd have to give up on it altogether, as well as start over on my profile."

"Well," Jake said, "Does this close the chapter on the Focus Film Society? Or is it going to be a regular thing for you now? You know, you and Terry and all your new friends?"

"Well, yes, I really do enjoy the film society. I was planning to continue to go to screenings," Nancy began, then she blinked as she became aware that Jake had stressed the word *Terry*. She realized then that Jake was actually jealous of Terry.

"Oh, Jake!" she exclaimed, surprised. "You're jealous!" Jake's face reddened, and Nancy smiled, pleased that he cared so much.

"I like Terry as a friend, but it doesn't come close to the way I feel about you," Nancy said as she put her arms around Jake. Jake's expression was one of relief.

"Well, that's good, because I feel pretty strongly about you," Jake said.

Nancy considered his words for a moment.

"Hey," she said. "Fall weekend is coming up right after exams. Why don't you come to River Heights with me? You could meet my dad and Hannah, she's our housekeeper, but she's really like a mother to me."

"Sounds serious," Jake said, his eyes locking deeply into hers.

"Oh, you never know. It just might be," Nancy said with a little laugh. Then she pulled Jake close and gave him a long, passionate kiss.

NEXT IN NANCY DREW ON CAMPUS™:

What's with Emmet anyway? Eileen just can't seem to figure the guy out. Great-looking, fun to be with, but just when the going is good, he's sure to say or do something guaranteed to kill the mood. And talking about awkward: The only thing Stephanie likes about her job is her manager, and she likes him a lot. Problem is, he may be running a major scam on the side. Maybe Nancy can get to the bottom of it . . . if she can find the time. She's got her hands full, running a scam of her own—on Jake! One of his articles has been picked up by the *Chicago Daily Herald,* and Nancy's planning a celebration. It'll involve secrecy, deception, maybe even a bit of melodrama, but if it works, it'll be a night Jake will never forget . . . in *Hard to Get,* Nancy Drew on Campus #14.

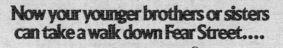